Potter School Newport (R.I.)

## Services at the Dedication of the School House

erected by the trustees of the Long wharf, May 20th, 1863

Potter School Newport (R.I.)

**Services at the Dedication of the School House**
*erected by the trustees of the Long wharf, May 20th, 1863*

ISBN/EAN: 9783337367442

Printed in Europe, USA, Canada, Australia, Japan

Cover: Foto ©Andreas Hilbeck / pixelio.de

More available books at **www.hansebooks.com**

# SERVICES

AT THE

# DEDICATION OF THE SCHOOL HOUSE

ERECTED BY THE

## 𝔗𝔯𝔲𝔰𝔱𝔢𝔢𝔰 𝔬𝔣 𝔱𝔥𝔢 𝔏𝔬𝔫𝔤 𝔚𝔥𝔞𝔯𝔣,

AT

# NEWPORT, RHODE ISLAND,

MAY 20th, 1863,

# WITH AN APPENDIX.

———•—◆—•———

NEWPORT:
PRINTED BY PRATT & MESSER.
1863.

# ADDRESSES

OF

# WILLIAM C. COZZENS,

*Governor of Rhode Island.*

# WILLIAM H. CRANSTON,

*Mayor of Newport,*

# A. HENRY DUMONT,

*Chairman of the Public School Committee,*

# HENRY ROUSMANIERE,

*Public School Commissioner.*

Delivered at the dedication of the " Trustees of the Long
Wharf School House," on the 20th of May, 1863.

22

# THE BOARD OF TRUSTEES OF LONG WHARF.

## ANNUAL MEETING APRIL 13TH, 1863,

#### WITH THE DATE OF THEIR ELECTION.

# INTRODUCTION.

The Trustees of the Long Wharf in Newport, having leased their wharf to the Newport & Fall River Railroad Company, who are now constructing a road from Newport to Fall River, to connect with the Old Colony Railroad to Boston, granting them for one hundred years (or more,) the entire use and control of said wharf, upon certain liberal conditions, specified in .contract (see Appendix); it seems a proper time for the Trustees to make a permanent and substantial demonstration towards carrying out that portion of the original designs of the Trust, in its formation in the year 1795, by erecting a Public School House and placing it in charge of the City Government.

In accordance therewith, they have erected a very fine, substantial edifice on the corner of Third and Willow Streets, in the first ward.

The lot upon which the building stands is one hundred feet square. The building fronts on Willow Street and measures fifty-four feet on that street, and forty feet on Third Street. It is built of pressed brick, the foundation and trimmings being of freestone, two stories high, with slate roof, making it fire proof, and of the most substantial character. The principal room in each story is fourteen feet in the clear and thirty-six and a half feet square, each room having seats for one hundred scholars, with ample room for all other purposes. There is also a recitation room in each story eleven by nineteen feet, amply provided with seats, &c. The rooms are well ventilated and very light, the windows being large, with glass three feet by two and a half. The halls and stairways are large and commodious. The furniture is of modern pattern, black walnut, and the seats and desks have iron ends. In the basement, which is ten feet in height, there is a good well of water, the floor is composed of concrete, well under-drained and perfectly dry. The apparatus for heating the building with steam is in the basement, and the heat is conducted through the building by pipes which are invisible, as they are placed between the ceiling and outside walls.

The architect was George C. Mason, the masonry was by John Freeborn, carpentering by Philip Simmons, painting by George W. Green & Co., and the furnishing by Ernest Goffe.

The building being completed and ready for occupancy on the first of June, the Trustees had previously voted that a celebration of the Trust and a dedication of the building should be observed with appropriate ceremonies. Whereupon His Excellency, William C. Cozzens, Governor of the State (one of the Trustees), was invited to deliver an address, commemorative of the event, placing the property in the hands of the Mayor and City Council. David G. Cook, Esq., Chairman of the Board, was invited to prepare an abstract from the records of the Trustees, to accompany the address, in pamphlet form, as an appendix; and Wednesday, May 20th, 1863, was appointed for the celebration. The Building Committee, Messrs. Samuel Engs, David J. Gould and Robert Sherman, with the addition of Charles E. Hammett, Jr., were appointed to make the necessary arrangement for the celebration, all which was done in an admirable manner; and to accommodate a larger audience than the commodious room on the lower floor would seat, a platform was erected outside the building, connected with the middle window, covered and decorated with our country's flag; the yard was filled with benches, and at two o'clock a large assemblage of people were present to witness the ceremonies. The inside of the house was occupied by the City Council, the School Committee, Clergy of the city, Teachers of the Public Schools, and many others, while a large number were seated on the outside, in the yard, and in the streets adjoining; the speakers and the reporters occupying the platform.

At 3 o'clock the assembly was called to order by David G. Cook, Esq., and a most impressive and appropriate prayer was offered by the Reverend Charles T. Brooks.

Governor Cozzens then delivered his address. The Chairman of the Board of Trustees presented the keys to His Honor, the Mayor, who responded and then presented the keys, with an appropriate address, to the Chairman of the School Committee. Doctor Dumont responded, after which Henry Rousmaniere, Esq., State School Commissioner, made an address, and with a benediction by the Rev. Wm. S. Child, Rector of Zion Church, these interesting services were brought to a close. The day was beautiful, and all present were able to hear the speakers and highly gratified with this valuable addition to our school accommodations.

# GOV. COZZENS' ADDRESS.

*Mr. Chairman, Mr. Mayor, and Fellow-Citizens:*

We have assembled this day, in and around this new and beautiful building, to dedicate it to the sacred cause of learning; to celebrate a Trust, conceived in the heart and mind of the merchants and philanthropists in the earlier days of our history. They have indeed passed away, and now slumber in yonder resting place, amid the countless throng who have gone before us.

It is right and proper that we should make this occasion one of general interest and rejoicing; not only for the object itself, but that we should, in thought and feeling, go back through generations of our ancestors, and stir up in our minds the noble deeds which actuated them.

The history of Newport is full of the reminiscences of the past, occupying, as it does, this portion of our beautiful island, from which the State takes it name. We grew up and flourished under our colonial connection with Great Britain, more prosperously than any of her towns or provinces. 'Our great and acknowledged natural advantages for trade and commerce, our splendid harbor and bay, our proximity to the ocean, ease of access with every wind and tide, have been the admiration of all time and of all nations, and are, even at this day, almost beyond comparison.

One hundred years ago, Newport was approaching her zenith, with a large and flourishing commerce, numberless manufactories, a great domestic and foreign trade, with merchant princes that outvied all other places on this Western Continent, the seat of learning and refinement; indeed, with every element to make a great, prosperous, and flourishing community. As far back as the year 1729, the celebrated Bishop Berkley,— whose arrival and stay at Newport have been so often chronicled in history, as connected with religious, historical, and literary events in our character,—attracted by our facilities for commerce, splendid climate and ocean scenery, wrote to his friend in Dublin that " The town of Newport is the most thriving place in all America for bigness. It is very pretty, and pleasantly situated. I was never more agreeably surprised than at the first sight of the town and harbor." At this time, it contained about 6000 inhabitants, and was rapidly increasing. From 1740 to the period of the Revolution, the commercial prosperity of Newport was unequalled. The statistics of our custom and import business, show an amount of value almost incredible. The history of those times corroborates the traditions of memory, handed down to us by our ancestors, of princely mansions and princely fortunes in and around this town, that make even much of these days dwindle into insignificance. The large and profitable business of those colonial times made many very rich, and all classes shared in the common prosperity; every trade and profession had its share, and Newport was rapidly securing its title of the Eden of America.

It was generally conceded that Newport had every advantage. Wealth had centred here, and was attracting capitalists from every part of the world. Between 1750 and 1760, some hundreds of wealthy Israelites, a most distinguished class of merchants, removed here from Spain, Portugal, Jamaica, and other places, and entered largely into business. One of them, Mr. Aaron Lopez, owned a large fleet of vessels (rising thirty at one time) in the foreign trade, and many more in the coasting trade. The order boxes,—or pigeon holes, as we sometimes call them,—with the names of his vessels on them, are still to be seen in one of the old stores on the Lopez (now Finch & Engs') Wharf. But I will not dwell on this now, but in the course of what I have to say, will present some facts showing more practically the extent of the business of this town previous to the revolutionary war. Every element of success was within our reach ; our imports attracted the attention of merchants from New York, Boston and Salem; indeed, from every place of note in the then American Colonies. We were growing rich and great, and building up a city, which, had it not been interrupted and destroyed by the war of the Revolution, might long ere this have covered this whole island, and been to-day the metropolis of this Western World. That, however, was not our fate; the very elements of prosperity which had built us up so early after the settlement of the country—our splendid harbor, and other facilities—were the first attractions of the war. We had rebelled against the usurpations of the mother country, and we suffered for it. We had no fortifications to rely upon, except Fort George (now Fort Walcott); that was unfinished, and we had no other means of defence. The devastations of that war upon this fated *town*, were far greater than upon any other, because of the importance of this harbor and bay as a depot and rendezvous for their ships-of-war—a fact acknowledged by all the powers of the earth, save only, perhaps, that of our own United States.

The natural consequence of this position was ruin to our merchants, our town was depopulated, several hundred stores and dwellings (some accounts say 480, some say 900) were burnt and otherwise destroyed. Every wharf built of wood was torn up for fuel. Houses, gardens, orchards, all were ruthlessly invaded, and every injury that could be done was done. But I will not enlarge upon it here. Our business to-day is with the Long Wharf in Newport. We meet to celebrate an *epoch* in its history. It is, and always has been, one of the institutions of the place, a public wharf. Its extreme length, its formation, bounded south on the harbor for nearly one-third of a mile, formed a more than usual interest by its general location for boats and for fishing, and its bridge-way, through which the tide has ebbed and flowed for near two hundred years. The first town record we find of it, as a Long Wharf, is April 29, 1685, when it is alluded to, in granting a privilege to build another wharf into the sea between the lands of John Tillinghast and others, on the same terms as the town had previously granted lands for the new Long Wharf. The record of this first grant is no doubt among the mutilated portions of our early history, that were under water so long at Hurlgate, near New York, and cannot be recovered.* This wharf has, therefore, naturally been the most important and popular among our many wharves, and its chequered history most interesting to our community. In the year 1702, we find efforts were made to rebuild it, it having suffered in severe gales, and was rapidly going to decay. It was then called the Old Town Wharf; and the town voted to offer it to certain persons, if they would repair it and keep it in order, collect the wharfage, and thus reimburse themselves for the outlay. At this time, March 16, 1702, the town voted rates of wharfage, etc., etc. Again, in December, 1702, the proprietors paid up their assessments, appointed a wharfinger, and again joined in the management of the wharf. In October, 1739, these former proprietors were not willing to widen and lengthen out the wharf, to meet the

* See Appendix A, relating to Town Records.

23

demands of commerce, unless they should have a vote of the town giving them the fee in said wharf, with certain other rights; whereupon the town voted the proprietors certain lands and flats westward of Easton's Point, so called, eight hundred feet in length and fifty feet in width, and from this time the Long Wharf began to assume its present length. The reason for this grant was thus expressed in their petition:—"For the benefit of the inhabitants according to the grant of the town, the lower part of said wharf will be commodious for the lying of larger vessels, which will greatly tend to encourage great commercial interests. The building out of said wharf will employ a vast number of tradesmen and other inhabitants, and when completed will, in addition to Queen street, (now the Parade,) form nearly three-quarters of a mile in length, exactly straight, and being in front of a magnificent Court House that is now erecting there at great expense; the beauty and grandeur of which, when completed, will appear the greatest in all New England, be advantageous to the public and private interest,—the committee being vested with power and authority to accomplish the said design in the best manner for the glory and ornament of the town and colony."

In the year 1746 the same proprietors obtained from the General Assembly authority to set up a Ferry between Newport and Jamestown, on certain conditions and restrictions, in regard to other grants previously made. They established the Ferry, and continued for some time to do a good business, although there were several other ferry lines at the same time.

In 1769 the proprietors again petitioned the General Assembly, representing that they were under covenant for building out 170 feet more, westerly, on said wharf, and that they had suffered very much by unexpected high tides, and by a disastrous fire consuming their warehouses, and asked a grant for a lottery, which was obtained, allowing them to raise the sum of thirteen hundred and fifty pounds lawful money.

Here let us stop for a while and examine the legislation of Rhode Island, on the subject of lotteries; for we find that from 1752 down to 1840, lotteries were one of the acknowledged and most popular modes of raising money. Petitions were made to the Legislature from every town in the State to raise money for every conceivable object, beginning in 1752, with a grant to raise means to pave streets in Newport; the next to build a fort on Goat Island, (Fort George, now Fort Walcott,) say £10,000. From this time, lotteries became a real mania with the people; every court house in the State, every church, every meeting house, or nearly so, parsonage houses, to pave streets, build wharves, establish libraries, make roads, protect fish, build bridges, build colleges, relieve bankrupt estates, and many private objects, all were aided in this way to a greater or less extent. Hundreds of thousands of dollars were allowed to be raised, and it would seem that every individual in the State must have participated in it, as we find citizens of the highest, most respectable and religious character, engaged as commissioners, or parties to it. Lotteries continued, without much abatement, down to 1806, having been countenanced and patronized for over half a century, without discovering the gambling character they were assuming. At this time, applications became so numerous, and many which were unauthorized being found in the market, that the Assembly passed a law to prosecute all that were not legal, but repealed it same year, next session. Not until 1840, January Session, did the Legislature fully realize their wicked and desperate character, when we find a resolution relating to the great evils they were entailing upon our State, morally and financially, and recommending their discontinuance. In 1845 stringent laws were passed relating to the sale of tickets. And now many years have passed since this State has allowed lotteries, or permitted traffic in them—a wise result, remedying a pernicious and expensive evil.

We now return to 1769 in the history of the Long Wharf. The amount raised by the lottery was expended on the wharf, and it continued to prosper until destroyed by the British in 1779. The lower part being mostly built of timber,—especially the west end,—it was burnt to the water's edge. Thus it remained through all the disheartening years of the war, a dilapidated shell, reflecting on its surface at low tide, the sad history of a broken down, destroyed, depopulated town, shorn of all its grandeur, its population reduced one-half with devastation and ruin in every step, the very elements of our former strength and power, everything that had contributed to our position and growth turned suddenly to our disadvantage, our nearness to the ocean, the fear of continued wars, our liability to be again and again destroyed, discouraged our capitalists, our business men. And from that time many of them, yes, a great many of them, and more especially those who had been tempted by our supposed advantages to adopt this as their home, now gathered up all they had left from the wreck of war, and leaving this their idolized and beautiful home by the side of the sea, retreated inland, or to less exposed places for business, and there devoted their energies free from all the discouraging sights, which our desolated place presented to their view. It is true a few of our old native-born distinguished merchants still remained, and though paralyzed in fortune and in spirit, they clung to their loved home, and endeavored to resuscitate their fallen fortunes and their unfortunate town. They met with some success, for in 1795 we find that thirty-six of our most honorable and distinguished merchants, then residents of Newport, associating themselves together as a Board of Trustees of the Long Wharf, proposing to make one more effort to rebuild this wharf that had been destroyed by the ravages of war, and by fire, and was being washed away. The wood and logs of which it was built that escaped the fire, though partly under water, were being carried off by the poor for fire-wood, and very soon it would have been back to its native condition, a mere shore. They petitioned the General Assembly for an Act of Incorporation as a Board of Trustees, and at the same session obtained a grant for a lottery to raise $25,000 towards rebuilding this Long Wharf, and for building a hotel, which was supposed would be needed and be profitable; and further representing that all profits arising from said wharf and hotel, should be appropriated to building one or more public free schools, in such manner as the Trustees may direct. Thus it appears that they had a twofold object, of rebuilding this ancient and once flourishing wharf, for the benefit of commerce, and to aid the great cause of education, by the support of public schools. It would seem, that the public notice of this Act of Incorporation and the grant for a lottery to rebuild the wharf and establish public schools, attracted the attention of one Simeon Potter, a resident of Swanzey in the State of Massachusetts, who generously made a gift of two lots of land, with a dwelling house and other buildings, on Easton's Point, in Newport, to be combined with the fund to be raised and established for public schools. In his deed of gift he uses the following most touching language: "Now I, the said Simeon Potter, moved by the regard I have for the good people of the said Town of Newport, and by the afflictions which they have suffered in the late war, and wishing to promote their rise and prosperity, and the education of their children of the present and succeeding generation, do hereby in consideration thereof, give, grant, &c., &c."* This liberal donation for the objects

* See his letter in Appendix, C.

above specified, was an act of kindness and benevolence worthy
of honorable mention. From the time of the gift until 1814,
the house was rented, and the income was spent on repairs and
betterments of the estate. During the years 1796 to 1800 the
wharf was rebuilt. The lottery yielded a handsome sum,
although the amount does not appear (probably about $12,000),
as one of the Treasurers books of that date cannot be found.
The Committee of the Trustees performed their duties most
honorably, in regard to rebuilding the wharf and the management of the lotteries, without any charge for services, receiving
the thanks of the Board of Trustees. Here let me refer to a
copy of the record of the doings of the Trustees, from 1795
down to this present date, which has been condensed, and prepared by one of the Board, David G. Cook, Esq., the present
highly respected Chairman of the Board of Trustees, which it
is proposed will accompany this address as an Appendix* and
will supply to a great extent any deficiency in the matter of
statistics in regard to the wharf since 1795, which may be
expected here. It will supply the names of all the Trustees,
and the time of their appointment, the report of the annual and
special meetings, in fact the entire record of this important
Trust, including an elaborate report made by the Hon. Wm. R.
Staples, late Judge of the Supreme Court of this State, to the
Trustees by their request in 1858, tracing the history, title and
rights of the Trustees in this valuable property. I mention
this so particularly, in this connexion, to account for any seem-
ing neglect on my part to explain and more fully represent the
doings of the Trustees from time to time. My part of the duty
being understood to be, to make the address with the public
history of the wharf, and its connection with the reputation and
business interests of the town. I most fully recommend the

---

* See Appendix, Note C.

report here alluded to as a valuable history of the wharf, showing the faithful observance of a Trust, its interest in public
schools, and the disposition of all concerned to make the wharf
useful, attractive and profitable.

In 1814, the Trustees by way of carrying out the conditions
of the Trust, and applying the gift of Mr. Potter, appointed a
committee to devise a plan for opening a free school for poor
children. They reported accommodations in the Potter House,
for a school of fifty or sixty scholars. At this time, they made
an estimate of the probable income for this purpose, and
decided to begin with twenty or thirty scholars, which was duly
organized; and thus was inaugurated the first public school
from this Long Wharf fund. Capt. Joseph Finch and his wife
undertook the charge of this school for a very moderate compensation. In 1815 we find a report from this committee saying that twenty-five of the boys had made much greater progress in their studies than was anticipated, and that the teachers
had done ample justice to their pupils. At the annual meeting,
1815, the committee was further instructed to enlarge the school
to accommodate forty scholars, and means were put in train to
obtain pupils from different parts of the town. The record
says, " that all may have an opportunity of experiencing the
happy effects of so valuable an institution." A School Committee was annually appointed, and the school continued to flourish
until 1829, when on the decease of Capt. Finch it was changed
to a school for smaller children, under the care of his widow,
which continued until 1832, when it was given up. Public
schools under the direction of the town were then fully established on a liberal and popular basis, and it was unnecessary to
continue this on its then limited scale. The house which had
been occupied, the gift of Mr. Potter, was ordered to be sold,
and the proceeds deposited in the Savings Bank, where it has

remained ever since, with its accumulations of interest, amounting, when withdrawn to aid in the erection of this edifice, to the
handsome sum of twenty-two hundred and ninety-three $\frac{38}{100}$
dollars.

The school we have just alluded to was held on Washington
Street, corner of Marsh Street, and was known as the Long
Wharf Free School. Among its scholars were some of the
smartest boys in town, making good sailors, smart captains, and
good merchants. Some, I know, have risen to position and
wealth, yes, even to eminence; and some are now among our
most enterprising and liberal citizens. I well remember this
school from 1820 to its close, and shall never forget the novel
and most peculiar method adopted to give notice of school-time.
The teacher, having been an old sea captain, was more accustomed to use his lungs than hand-bells, and as there was no bell
belonging to the school, the teacher with great punctuality
would go first to the west window on Washington Street (second story), and call out at the top of his voice—and that voice
was not weak or delicate—three times, "Boys! Boys! Boys!"
Then he would appear at another window on the east side of
the house, and repeat the same call—"Boys! Boys! Boys!"
This being on the side of the cove, with buildings on all four
sides, forming a hollow square at least a thousand feet across,
over the water, it would at times produce a most prodigious
noise, heard as far almost as a steam whistle in these days. I
have often heard it, in my boyhood days, while sailing about
the cove in a boat, echo in every direction, east, north, south,
and west. Sometimes the second and third call would catch
the echo of the first, and with the roguish boys in their boat
joining in the general chorus, shouting at the top of their voices,
"Boys," too. Thus on many a bright morning, with a calm,
clear, atmosphere, has there been a confusion of sounds over

that, at times, crystal sheet of water, far surpassing the efforts of the most gifted ventriloquist. What effect these interferences of the boys, or the echoes, had upon the old schoolmaster's disposition and temper, I never heard. His voice has long been silent, but the echo of other voices can still occasionally be heard on that same cove, although very soon the whistle of the locomotive will take its place, and the cove, with all its associations, will be converted into a railroad station, an evidence of progress long desired.

Before we leave the matter of Public Schools, let us go back in history, and see what was done by our ancestors, the early settlers on this island, towards establishing popular education, now so universally appreciated in this country. I find that almost immediately after the settlement of the island, one Robert Lenthal was admitted a freeman by the General Court; and by a vote of the Town of Newport, August 6, 1640, was called to keep a public school for the learning of youth; and for his encouragement, there was granted to him one hundred acres of land, and four more acres for a house lot; and it was also voted that one hundred acres more should be laid forth and appropriated for a school for the encouragement of the poorer sort, to train up in learning; and Mr. Robert Lenthal, while he continues to teach school, is to have the benefit of said land. In Judge Staples' Annals of Providence, I find the first movement made in Providence, was May 9, 1663, when a grant of land was made for that purpose of one hundred acres of upland and six acres of meadow. The first schoolmaster in Providence was one William Turpin, who was there in 1684. But their schools did not appear to have made much progress until 1750, and upwards. In 1697, April 28, Newport voted other school lands for the benefit of a schoolmaster. In 1704, the town built another school house at the public charge. The vote

24

describes place, size, &c. The town voted six acres of land to be sold, proceeds to be used towards building the school house. Also a tax of one hundred and fifty pounds for same object. Another vote that the inhabitants living to the north and near Middletown, shall not be liable to said tax, because they lived too far off to send their children. Some delays were occasioned by the difficulty of selling the land and deciding upon the location; but a large and commodious school house was finally built and finished August 18, 1709, Mr. William Gilbert chosen schoolmaster, to have the benefit of the school lands for one year. Here, again, is evidence of the progress of knowledge. At a town meeting, October 4, 1710, a very respectful petition from a Mr. Galloway, for the liberty of teaching a Latin School in the two little rooms in the school house, is hereby granted.

October 7, 1713, the town voted to establish another school, and Benjamin Nicholson was chosen schoolmaster. A committee was also appointed to repair the town school house. July 28, 1714, John Hammett was chosen a schoolmaster to officiate in this office for nine years, on the same terms as others have been paid. January 29, 1723, a further petition for a school house in the eastern portion of the town voted 106 acres of land for that purpose. Again, January 25, 1726, in town meeting,— "Whereas, there are some buildings in town, improved for schools, which are of great advantage to the public, which, unless repaired, will become useless, and particularly the great school house, it is ordered that all the public school houses in the precincts of Newport be repaired, and paid for out of the public treasury." It will appear by the foregoing extracts from our town records, that Newport was really a pioneer in the establishment of public schools. I know of no place where public schools were established so early after the settlement of the country, and on so liberal a scale. I find no time on our records when education was not a very important subject in our town legislation. It has, of course, like all other important objects, expanded in our prosperity and suffered by our adversity. From 1726 down to the time of the revolution, we find the same devotion to the cause of learning that characterized our early settlers; but evidently, private schools monopolized a large share of the youth between 1740 and 1776, as their parents were in a flourishing business, and could well afford to educate them according to their choice.

From 1776 down to 1825, but very little interest was manifested in public, or even private schools. The disheartening influences of the war had paralyzed every effort, and many had lost all their property, or nearly all, with a prospect of heavy burdens and taxes. The school houses were turned into barracks, and were literally used up by the enemy in possession of the town. Consequently, public schools appear to have been abandoned, and we discover no evidence of any effort being made to restore them, until 1825. Thus it appears that the only public school existing in the town during that time was the Long Wharf Free School, supported by the Trust we this day celebrate. Some private schools were established, and did good service; but the spirit of former days had departed, and each child had to depend for an education on the ability of its parents; most of them were well educated for those times, as the expense was comparatively small. Indeed, had the present high prices of living existed in those days, with no more business than we had then, we should, as was often said of us, long since have eaten ourselves up. Since 1830 public schools have again revived, and on a most permanent and substantial basis, and at this time are equal to any in New England. I will not weary you with any particulars, they are familiar to all I ad-

dress to-day, and in closing my review of public schools, I feel
proud to own them as a great element in our present character.

Having traced the history of the Long Wharf, and fully identified it with the history of Newport, in an important commercial
point of view; having also furnished you with considerable evidence that Newport has, from her earliest settlement, been seri-
ously devoted to public schools and popular education, which
will in a measure account for so much being said in history
about this ancient seat of learning, social refinement, &c;
there can be no doubt, that while so much was done to educate
the poorer classes, the richer class must have had superior
schools for those early days.

The Trust we celebrate to-day, is the Long Wharf and Public Schools, identical heretofore, inseparable hereafter. While
I have wandered through the records and histories of Newport,
to cull whatever seems appropriate to the object of this celebration, I have found much beyond the immediate object of this
Trust, which, I doubt not, may be interesting to you, and to those
who may come after us. I shall therefore trespass upon your
patience while I relate some of those evidences or indications
of that early, high commercial character of Newport, during
the last century, and the causes of her decline; rescuing, perhaps, some things in history from being lost sight of. I find
much that is interesting, but the further limits of this address will allow me only a brief recital. The earlier history
of Newport and of Rhode Island, as regards its first settlement,
its religious character, its contests for freedom to worship God,
and all the trials of its early life, have been often and most
elaborately presented, forming an interesting epitome of the
history of this State. An eminent historian* once said, " The
annals of Rhode Island, if written in the spirit of philosophy,

---

*Hon. George Bancroft.

would exhibit the forms of society under a peculiar aspect. Had the territory of the State corresponded to the importance and singularity of the principles of its early existence, the world would have been filled with wonder at the phenomena of its early history."

I shall therefore proceed at once to exhibit such evidences of our commercial character as I have been able to gather from the storehouse of history, adopting only a few illustrations, lest I should weary you and extend this address to an unreasonable length. From the year 1700, the infancy of these then British Colonies, Newport began to enjoy a most successful distinction in attracting the attention of men of wealth and character. It seemed designed by nature and position, to develop advantages for commerce and manufacturing which few places then possessed, and from 1729 to 1742 a very considerable business was done, both in navigation and manufacturing; but no particular history of those days is left us; what once existed, was lost forever in the whirlpool of the revolution. One evidence of a large shipping interest may be inferred from the establishment of the Newport Marine Society, which originated in 1752 and was incorporated in 1754, under the name of the Fellowship Club, and continued to bear that name until 1785, when it was changed to the Marine Society. During the first eight years of this Society from 1752 to 1760, one hundred and twenty-five sea captains were admitted members, showing a large commerce; from that time to 1800, one hundred and thirty-six more members, and since then, a period of sixty-three years, only about one hundred and fifty more. During the one hundred and eleven years since its organization, this society has been most honorably sustained, and has, to-day, a safely invested fund of $20,000; the entire income is regularly distributed to the widows and orphans of deceased members, and every dollar of

its income is applied to its legitimate uses, in aid of the poor
and unfortunate.

From our Custom House records, it appears that, during the
year 1763, there were 184 vessels cleared on foreign voyages,
360 odd in the coasting trade, a large number of fishing vessels,
and besides these a regular line of London packets. Two-
thirds of all these vessels were owned in Newport, requiring a
regular force of 2,200 seamen. Every year from this time the
shipping was increasing. In 1769, Newport appears to have
been at the height of her prosperity. The entries of arrivals
at the Custom House, during the two months of July and August,
were 64 vessels from foreign voyages, 17 whalemen, 134 coast-
wise. During the next three months among many other arrivals
were 16 cargoes of molasses, bringing over 3,000 hhds. These
vessels were all owned in Newport, and their cargoes were
imported here for manufacturing purposes. Many such cases
might be quoted, but this is enough to give an idea of the
commerce of that day. Now let us look at the business which
required so much shipping. The manufacture of sperm oil and
candles was introduced into Newport by the Jews, from Lisbon,
between 1745 and 1750, and from that time to 1760 there were
put in full operation 17 factories for these articles alone; also
22 distilleries, 4 sugar refineries, 5 ropewalks, and many large
furniture factories, shipping immense quanties of furniture to
New York, the West Indies, Surinam, and many other places.
In 1770 I find mention made of eighteen West India vessels
arriving here in one day. The great central position of these
factories and distilleries was in and around the vicinity of the
Cove and Long Wharf. At one time there were seven wharves,
eleven distilleries and several shipyards in the Cove. Many
vessels were built therein, some of considerable size; one rather
celebrated sloop called the *Rising Sun*, was built by one Gideon

Davenport. All vessels built in the Cove, as well as those landing their cargoes there, passed through the bridge, which then had a commodious draw twenty-six feet wide. About this time an effort was made to render the running tide in and out of the Cove, available for power to run a mill. The privilege was granted to John Hadwen, but I cannot find it ever amounted to much. Another effort was made many years after with no better success.

About the year 1770 the population of the town was said to be not less than twelve thousand; with at least two hundred vessels in the foreign trade, and four hundred in the coasting trade, all owned in Newport.*

During this period in our history I see no mention made of Insurance Companies. (First in this State was in 1799, one in Newport, one in Providence.) Our merchants had to stand their own underwriters, and some years they met with most disastrous results; one year in particular, there were a great many shipwrecks, with loss of vessels and cargoes, and a great loss of life, making, it is said, at least two hundred widows in one year.

At this time, Newport was decidedly ahead of New York in her foreign and domestic trade. Aaron Lopez, whom I have before alluded to, with Godfrey Malbone, Henry Collins, the Brinleys, Wantons, and many others, were among the largest ship owners and heaviest merchants; but the number of those owning ten or twelve vessels and doing a large business, is perfectly incredible. Pardon me if I step aside to relate an incident which has been current for nearly a century, and worthy to be handed down as a specimen of old fashioned shrewdness. Old Christopher Almy, a Merchant of those days, having had a cargo of molasses landed on his wharf, now called the old Ham-

* See Historical Memoranda, Appendix A.

mond Wharf, ordered one of his negroes to watch it at night
(they had slaves here at that time), and during one of the
nights, to try his faithfulness, he visited the wharf himself and
began to reconnoitre among the casks to draw some molasses,
when discovered by his faithful servant he endeavored to escape,
but being caught by him, Mr. Almy used every means to con-
vince the negro that he was his master; but it was of no avail,
the watchman was inexorable and admitted no such plea.   No
sir, said he, my massa no such fool as dat, to come down here
dis time of night to steal his own molasses; and he therefore
proved his capacity to guard the property intrusted to his care
by dispatching the old man into the dock.   His faithfulness no
doubt satisfied Mr. Almy, but his treatment was rather a
damper.

One more anecdote which is equally well authenticated, let
me relate, in passing, as it refers to about these times, showing
such a striking difference between Providence and Newport,
less than a hundred years ago, while Newport was engaged in
the extensive business we have been describing, and enjoying
that high position in the American colonies.   When the merchant from New York visited Newport to purchase goods
imported here, and wrote home to his wife saying what a large
and thriving place Newport was, expressing his hope that some
day "New York may rival Newport," then it was that Newport
was importing thousands of hogsheads of molasses per month,
and a goodly portion of it was landed on this Long Wharf.
Occasionally the Newport packet plying between here and
Providence would take from this said wharf a hogshead of this
good molasses, and, waiting a favoring breeze, start for Providence.   On her arrival there the town crier would be employed
to perambulate their streets ringing his bell at every corner, and
announcing that the sloop *Polly* had arrived from Newport with

a cask of most excellent molasses that would be retailed out on board said sloop at —— price per gallon, and inviting all those in want of some of it, to apply on board said sloop, before nine o'clock the following day.   I have this story related to me by a near relative of one,* who, not many years ago, at a ripe old age, honored and respected by everybody in Newport, his birth place, as well as in Providence where he had lived eighty odd years of his life, had often said that from the time of that announcement by the crier, he had seen people of all ages and sizes passing out of their houses and gateways with rundlets, jugs, and kettles, wending their way to the Newport packet to secure a portion of this delicious top-dressing for their cakes.   I mention this story only to show the primitive way in which things were done in comparison with Newport, even in places that since that time have outgrown us in everything that constitutes a flourishing community.

Between the years 1770 and 1776, while our wharves and harbor were filled with vessels laden with merchandise from every part of the world, and everything was going on prosperously, many English war vessels were sent here to aid in enforcing the revenue laws, which had become very stringent and obnoxious to our people, and were being daily resisted.   At one time in 1774, a whole fleet lay at anchor in our harbor. From this time the incidents of the revolution surrounded us. Such was our unfortunate position that our commerce, our manufactures, and all the elements of a growing prosperity, made us, of course, the chief object of attack.   England became jealous of our success, and inflamed at our boldness and independence—witness the destruction of His Majesty's sloop Liberty in our harbor, 1769, and the Gaspee on the river, near Providence, in 1772.   From this time we were closely watched

* The venerable John Howland.

and guarded by some of their most powerful forces intended to
intimidate us. On the 20th July, 1776, they threatened to
bombard the town. Making preparations by the ships taking
their position, they put quantities of tar and other inflammable
matter into the ferry boats, in order as it was said, to set fire
to the town. After keeping up the alarm two days, they left
the harbor and sailed on a cruise. Great numbers of the inhabitants of the town, removed about this time, taking all they
could carry with them. Thus surrounded by ships-of-war, we
continued to assert our independence till December, 1776, when
the large British fleet arrived, commanded by Sir Peter Parker,
with an army of ten thousand men, English and Hessians, who
immediately took us captive, landing his army in the midst of
this community, creating a consternation that can be more easily
imagined than described. From this time our destruction commenced. They burnt our factories and our ships, tore up our
wharves, stores, and warehouses, depopulated our town, and
occupied or mutilated everything around us.

In July, 1778, a French fleet, consisting of eleven ships-of-
the-line, besides frigates and transports, under the command of
Count D'Estaing, arrived in our harbor and outside. These,
with the English frigates and ships, must have made exciting
times in our harbor and bay.

In 1778, November 12th, twelve more British ships and frigates arrived.

About the 1st of October, 1779, there were indications of
an evacuation of the Island of Rhode Island. On the 11th, a
fleet of fifty-two sail of transports arrived, and took off seven
thousand men and all their ordnance and military stores. On
their leaving, they burnt and destroyed everything within their
reach. The records of these times are filled with the distress
which pervaded all things about us.

In 1780, July 10th, another French fleet, consisting of forty-four men-of-war and transports, under Admiral De Terney, having on board six thousand troops, arrived from France. The next day the troops landed, and were put in possession of the forts. The arrival of this fleet inspired the people with new life; and although they were frequently exposed and liable to renewed attacks from the English fleets, nothing more was attempted. The history of these events, and these times, is deeply interesting, but my time will not permit any further notice.

Between 1776 and 1782 the effects of the war and its probable future upon the success of our people, reduced our population one-half in numbers, and at least two-thirds in reality, as those who left here were best able to establish themselves elsewhere, leaving behind the poor and the ruined as a burden upon the town. With this sad picture staring our people in the face, with desolation stamped upon everything within us and around us, but few had the heart and the energy to enjoy even the glad tidings of the peace of 1783. For nearly ten years had we been a prey to the invasions of a foreign foe, and were becoming accustomed to it. Yet peace was a great relief; the few of our distinguished merchants who remained, gathered up the fragments that were left, and once more started on a career of business, but it came hard, the spirit was broken; the charms of prosperity had vanished, still they struggled on. There was a considerable revival of business. Gibbs & Channing, and several others had embarked in new enterprises and were flourishing, when, lo, again the sound of war reached our shores. Many of those who had passed through the Revolution were still alive and saw again in the sure future another devastation, and so it proved. The embargo of 1808 was the precursor, suspending all business. We again suffered; our people became disheartened; threatened with all the horrors of the former war, our town showed signs of again being invaded. In June, 1814 the General Assembly passed an Act authorizing the Town Councils of the seaport towns to cause their shipping to be removed from their wharves. The Council of Newport ordered the shipping here to be all removed from the wharves, lest it should be an inducement for the enemy to visit Newport again. Many of the vessels were sent up the river as far as they could go, and a great many of our citizens packed up all their valuables, in clothing, furniture, &c., our traders their merchandise, our bankers their banks, our Town Council their records, which were sent up the river or across the bay to more inland places, remembering how their fathers suffered in the war of 1776. This state of excitement was sooner relieved than was expected. The fourteenth of February, 1815, will forever be remembered by many now present when the blessed messenger of peace reached our town. Every demonstration of joy was evinced; our citizens began to breathe more freely; they had suffered much, yet they looked upon war as ever fatal to their prosperity and depressing to their minds.

This very year, that had given us a peace, also brought us a flood, with the ever memorable September gale, which occurred on the 23d of September, 1815, and which added greatly to our distress, doing an immense damage to our shipping, destroying many of our wharves, with the old stores that had survived the Revolution. The wreck of a great many of these old wharves is still visible, at low tide, frequently grounding vessels and boats as they approach our present docks. The tide daily ebbs and flows over numerous wharves, that one hundred years ago were loaded with merchandise. The Long Wharf suffered greatly in this gale.*

From this period to the year 1832, Newport was gradually

*See appendix C.

wasting away. There were still a few merchants left, who kept up a moderate business in commerce, and two or three distilleries, but otherwise, there was nothing doing. Scarcely a new building was erected between 1808 and 1832, save the new Asylum for the Poor, in 1819, on Coasters' Harbor Island. A few occasional spasms kept us alive. Our ship owners gradually ran out, whaling languished, our packet system was superseded by the steam power of other places, and we were being frittered away. Our young men were really the only article of export to any extent, and it is universally conceded that our contributions of this sort, to larger and more prosperous communities, was very great. We see the Newport element largely prevailing in many of the towns and cities around us. All of you will recollect the re-union of 1859. What multitudes of the native-born returned, on that ever-to-be-remembered jubilee, to join with their parents and friends, whom some of them had long since left. It is a source of sincere gratification, that so many of them are occupying honorable and responsible positions in their adopted homes; and while they may have a veneration for the home of their youth, the discouragement of their boyhood days naturally dwells upon their minds, weaning many of them most effectually from that love of their birth-place which a more prosperous condition would have given them. This is true. I have seen many coming home and comparing the energy and business of their new homes with ours; and they and their children have lived long enough to wonder at our want of enterprise, forgetting the causes that had weighed us down.

The war, now raging with such unparalleled wickedness, over many portions of our once happy country, is producing the same terrible consequences on the enterprise and prosperity of many of the once flourishing cities of the South, such as we experienced in the war of the Revolution. I will only instance New Orleans, in which I see a duplicate of the sad fate that overtook Newport. From having a levee, full three miles in length, piled up with merchandise and their great staples, with three, and often four hundred ships and many steamboats, all loading or unloading their valuable cargoes, what do we read? That business is suspended; there are no ships, and but few steamboats, except those engaged in the war. The business of a month now, does not equal the business of a day two years ago. A late writer says, " Our little business consists of a few hogsheads of sugar, a few barrels of molasses." With no heart for trade, their only hope may be, that when peace shall once more smile upon them, that the greater recuperative power of these times may save them and restore their trade.

I have trespassed, I fear, upon your patience, and upon the original object of this address, but finding the history of the Long Wharf so closely identified with the history of Newport, I could not well separate the two.

In every town or city there are some trusts or gifts of a public nature, designed by benevolent and liberal minds, to carry out or perpetuate some favorite object, looking forward to results long, perhaps, after they may have passed away; reflecting, oftentimes, in judicious care, consequences far more important than their authors had ever imagined. Such may be the case before us. The Long Wharf, in Newport, originating first in the 17th century, was improved and enlarged in 1702, by way of promoting the business of the colony and rendering aid to commerce; again, at sundry times, enlarged and rebuilt, until 1796, when the Trust we this day celebrate was formed; and after nearly seventy years under this organization, and almost two centuries of existence, subject to all the vicissitudes and changes of time, we are happy to announce its triumphant entrance upon a new career of usefulness and prosperity, with a new lease of life upon a responsible basis, a contract* having been completed with the Newport and Fall River Railroad Company for the entire control of said wharf, and the rights and privileges of said Trust Corporation, with liberty to enlarge and improve it in any way they please, at their own expense; the said wharf to be continued in good order and at an annual payment of fourteen hundred dollars, which amount (less some small expenses) will be forever hereafter appropriated to the cause of education.

It has been often said "that men cannot live after they are dead by controlling what they leave behind;" this is true to a great extent, but men can live in the everlasting gratitude of their fellow-men by a generous disposition of the means that God has given them; by a liberal founding of some institution of learning or some public benefaction by which their names may be continued in perpetual remembrance by all who come after them. Such is the case of many of those who have been our citizens; and the name of a Redwood, a Collins, a Touro, a King,† and many others, some of whom have slept for a century, are this day thought of and their noble deeds dwell upon our minds as we celebrate this Trust. As our country increases, and with it an ability to do good, we should encourage a liberal spirit by guarding with paternal care every trust committed to our keeping.

This Long Wharf Trust is now established upon a basis that we hope will endure for ages. If I could look with a prophetic eye into the future and see even this first lease with its one hundred and forty thousand dollars expended in Public School Houses and education (a result of this Trust), how gladly would I now hold it up to your view, but by a wise Providence that

* See Appendix C.    † See Appendix, Note B.

privilege is not allowed to mortal man, and happier far are we
that it is not.

And now, fellow-citizens, we have passed in review the history
of Newport since the year 1700, in regard to her business character, her prospects, her adversities, with its various changes,
and to-day we find ourselves engaged in the interesting duty of
dedicating this, edifice to the high and noble purpose for which
it was erected. We hail it as an auspicious epoch in our present history. I hope and trust we are on the eve of an important change in the prosperity and character of Newport; those
halycon days, which from my earliest recollections have been the,
theme of our constant and unceasing prayers, are beginning to
appear. In the adversities and vicisitudes of war, our people
lost faith in themselves and almost in their God, and were looking forward with anxious solicitude for "somebody" to build us
up and set us agoing. I see before me many of our citizens, who
can well remember much that I refer to, having lived the allot-
ted period of man's life, three score years and ten, and even
some yet in their strength who are approaching fourscore years.
Yours, my friends, has been a checkered and eventful life; coming on the stage of action at that unfortunate and unhappy
period in our history when the ravages and desolations of war
had laid portions of your beautiful home in ashes, sacrificing all
the accumulations of your fathers, prostrating every enterprise
and encouragement to persevere. You naturally partook of its
depression and have lived through a long life trusting in "Hope"
(the acknowledged and appropriate motto of our State) that you
may live to see the dawn of a sure prosperity, in which your
descendants (if not yourselves) may realize, amid the unsurpas-
sed surroundings of your island home, opportunities for business
and success such as this town once before enjoyed. The railroad, destined soon to connect us with the rest of the world, we

hope will do its part; it will save us from that complete isolation which has sometimes befallen us; it will give us many of those advantages which have built up other places; it will put us in direct and more reliable communication with Boston, the great central city of New England, and give us facilities for reaching New York, also by railroad. It will help our commerce, bring to us men of capital to enjoy the thousand blessings which are our portion here, and which have been the admiration of the seeker for health or pleasure for more than a century.

A late distinguished scholar and orator* of Providence, some twenty years ago, while delivering an address before the Legislature and people of Rhode Island, in speaking of Newport, its general and political character, says—" What touching memories does it awaken of the venerated and heroic dead, who once adorned this ancient seat of wealth, and talent, and social elegance, and who now slumber amid these scenes of placid and imperishable beauty." Again, he says—" In the vicissitudes of human affairs, Newport has declined from her ancient wealth and splendor; but within her and around her are left sources of enjoyment which mock the power of time and of change,—the living spirit of beauty which pervades her hills and vales,—the eternal sublimities which dwell around her shores."

God speed the time when Newport, with all these surroundings, may, in the future vicissitudes of human affairs, again assume those early days of wealth and splendor; and, amid the attractions which live within her, may we not hope that we shall catch the inspiration of the past, the renewed motive power of the present, developing in a successful future this beautiful island, studded all over with cottages and palaces—the happy home of a free, enterprising, virtuous, and heaven-protected people.

* Hon. Wm. G. Goddard, a Professor in Brown University.

26

At the conclusion of the foregoing address, Gov. Cozzens turned to His Honor, Mayor Cranston, and the City Council, and spoke as follows:

*Mr. Mayor and Gentlemen of the City Council :*

In the year 1795, thirty-six of the most distinguished merchants of Newport, forming a voluntary association, united in a petition to the General Assembly of the State, representing that the Long Wharf in Newport having been destroyed during the war of the Revolution, was lying waste, and trusting that in time the business of the place may be in some measure restored, asking authority as a Board of Trustees to raise by lottery (the popular and universal way to raise money in those days) the sum of $25,000 to aid in rebuilding said wharf and build a hotel; proposing that all rents and profits that should accrue from said Trust, should be devoted to public schools in Newport. In 1798, the town voted their rights in said wharf to the Trustees; the General Assembly made the grant; the organization was perfected; in time, the wharf was rebuilt. The amount raised by the lottery was not sufficient to build the hotel, nor was it needed, the principal income being required to finish the wharf, and has ever since been expended in widening and improving the property. A small public school was supported by the Trustees from 1815 to 1832, in the house given to the Trustees by Mr. Simeon Potter. At this time, the town having fully established public schools, this school was abandoned. Since then many improvements have been made to the wharf, and to-day the present Trustees have invited you to participate with them in this celebration, and in dedicating this new and substantial edifice to the sacred cause of learning. We have erected it as a memorial in honor of those distinguished men (long since deceased) who originated this Trust, and to those who have since aided in carrying out their benevolent designs.

We, their successors, to-day, rejoice to meet you in this beautiful building and offer you its free use and occupancy so long as it may be required for the purposes of education. We hold that Trust in perpetual succession, and propose to continue our organization, and to expend our means for the noble objects designed by its founders in such a way as will best subserve the cause of public schools, the requirements of the city, and do honor to the memory of all who have so faithfully devoted themselves to promote this most worthy object.

The Trustees have lately executed a lease of their wharf to the Newport and Fall River Railroad Company for one hundred years, with the privilege of further renewal, the lessees to keep it in repair, and make all such improvements as their business may require at their own expense, free from any cost to the Trustees. So that hereafter, Mr. Mayor, when this building shall all be paid for, we shall have over twelve hundred dollars a year to devote to the general objects of education.

I have, therefore, the pleasure to inform you that the Chairman of the Board of Trustees will now place in your hands the keys of this beautiful School House, with all its completeness, trusting it will ever receive the liberal care of the City Government and School Committee of Newport, and prove a valuable addition to the school accommodations of our city.

### · PRESENTATION OF KEYS.

D. G. Cook, Esq., then presented the keys to His Honor, Mayor Cranston, with the following remarks:

The Trustees of the Long Wharf, by their vote, have authorized and requested me, as their Chairman, to place in your hands the keys of this building, which duty it now gives me pleasure to perform.

# RESPONSE OF MAYOR CRANSTON.

*Gov. Cozzens, Mr. Chairman, and Gentlemen of the Board of Trustees of the Long Wharf:*

In behalf of the City Council I receive from your Chairman the keys of the noble and well arranged Public School House in which we are assembled. You, as well as your predecessors, are entitled to the thanks of the community for the faithful manner in which your duties have been gratuitously discharged for nearly three-quarters of a century. This building, so architecturally beautiful, and so admirably adapted in all respects for the important purpose for which it is hereafter to be used, will always be a proud monument, attesting the fidelity and liberality of the Trustees, and at the same time, be the educational home where thousands of tender minds will be cultivated and prepared for usefulness in all the duties of future life. Thus I receive it in behalf of the city, and thank you and your associates for all your disinterested labor. Your interesting account of the Trusteeship will be a valuable contribution to the history of our ancient city.

In proportion as the children are properly educated, will the men and women of each generation be ennobled; as the mind is judiciously cultivated, so is the heart purified, the soul enriched, and the men and women made nobler instruments of God on earth for the accomplishment of his original creative plans. Life is the great alembic in which all the elements of human character are being severely tried; and the result of this last great and fearful test will depend very materially upon how the children are educated, and what use they make of that education. We shall hereafter be, in a measure, responsible for the nature and extent of the means which we provide for this purpose; and the recipients will be equally answerable for the manner in which they use the result of those means. Let us earnestly hope that during long years to come, those who are instructed within these walls, will so improve their rich opportunities, as to enable them to enter upon the active duties of life, with the firm purpose to be faithful in all things, and ever continue useful members of society.

At the conclusion of these remarks, Mayor Cranston turned to the Rev. A. H. Dumont, D. D., Chairman of the Public School Committee, and addressed him as follows:

*Mr. Chairman and Gentlemen of the Public School Committee:*

Having received the keys of this noble edifice from the Trustees of the Long Wharf, by whose faithfulness and magnificence it has been erected, it is my duty now, in behalf of the City Council, to deliver them to you. This substantial and admirably arranged building is to be used hereafter for educational purposes, under the management of you and your successors, for years to come. You and your predecessors have labored earnestly, faithfully and gratuitously, for many years, in advancing the cause of education, and training the minds of children, from early youth to early manhood,—and thus preparing them to enter properly upon the discharge of the duties which they but indefinitely anticipate, but which we fully realize from experience.

A substantial education is the only solid basis upon which human character, in its noblest and most useful development, can be established; educate the masses plainly, substantially and thoroughly,—teach them to love God and fear his displeasure,—to obey willingly all laws, whether divine or human, and forever be loyal on earth,—and there will be a race who will fully comply with the divine requirements, especially for peace on earth and good will among men.

The character of the people of this country, for generations to come, is daily being moulded and formed in the Public Schools and the Sabbath Schools; these invaluable Institutions are the great earthly nurseries where these seeds of hope and promise, these buds of immortality, are being expanded and ripened into maturity, and prepared for that new garden of Eden where the tempter and destroyer can never enter. The responsibility of those to whom these children are entrusted, for the formation and cultivation of their minds, is great and fearful indeed. The hearts, as well as the intellects, of the children should be carefully and thoroughly educated. If you train only the mind—if you perfect that, as far as perfection can exist on earth, and neglect the cultivation of the heart,—neglect the Bible, neglect the Sabbath School, and desecrate God's holy day of rest,— you may raise a nation of intellectual giants, but it will be a nation of moral monsters, whose acts, deeds, and influences will equal, if not exceed, those who lived on earth before the deluge. There is no vice which is so potent and terrible, there is no licentiousness which is so captivating, desolating, and fatal, as that which emanates from a strong and polished mind, which recognizes no power above its own, no paradise but earth, and no pleasure but that which is of the passing moment. If the people of this country should ever be of that class, a more fearful doom awaits us than that which

befel the ancient cities of the East. As you purify and ethereal-
ize the individual, so do you elevate and ennoble the national
character. There are national as well as individual sins; and
the great Judge of the universe will punish the one as well as
the other. Childhood· is the sweet and happy portion of our
lives; then only little clouds hover over the delicate brow, and
but trifling troubles perplex the tender mind. These buds of
innocence have scarcely a care or responsibility, and when the
pleasures of the day are over, they lay their weary forms to
rest, and are soon lost in slumber, while their souls wander to
a beautiful dream-land, where all is fragrant as the blossoming
Spring. In the morning they awake, as the early notes of the
birds, which are God's little messengers of love and harmony,
are breaking upon their ears, making the air melodious with
echoes, as it were, of the perfect music of the new Paradise—
and arise with the sun, refreshed by repose, and with light and
glad hearts commence the duties of the day. Thus they pass
the early morning of life, until they gradually approach the
years of manhood, when cares surround them and anxieties
perplex them. Then the whole scene is changed, for they
commence the arduous and responsible duties which are imposed
on all,—and they must perform their part in the great and
thrilling drama of human life. The formation of the character .
is the most important and responsible trust that is confided to
parents, guardians, and teachers; and those who execute it with
scrupulous fidelity, discharge an onerous duty for which they
will be rewarded hereafter in that better land where there will
be but one infallible Teacher and one perfect school.

Into your hands, Mr. Chairman, I deliver these keys, and to
you, your associates and successors, entrust this building, with
entire confidence that the generosity of the donors will be fully
appreciated by all parties interested, and the rich fruits of that
generosity enjoyed by generations to come.

Response of Rev. A. H. Dumont, Chairman of Public School
Committee:

*Mr. Mayor and Gentlemen of the City Council:*

Among the difficulties which have, at times, surrounded the
School Committee, and have hindered their efforts to promote
the best interests of the Public Schools, not the least has been
that of procuring school-rooms in proper locations, and adequate
to the needs which existed.    To this general rule this section of
our city has been no exception.

The inconvenient place, now and for some years, used by the
schools of this district, was, at its first occupancy, hailed by the
Committee and the people as a very great advance on any previous accommodation.    You may easily fancy, sir, what was the
gratification and what was, I may add, the gratitude of the Committee and of the inhabitants of this Ward, when it was
announced that the Trustees of the Long Wharf intended to
erect a convenient and beautiful house for their accommodation.

And now, to-day, when we here behold the full execution of
that purpose carried out with so much taste and such large liberality; and looking forward, as we well may, to results, which,
under the blessing of God, we have a right to expect, we may
well be pardoned if our emotions are too mighty for utterance.

Philanthropists, who, for successive years, are brought into
constant intercourse with young minds in their course of education, and who have culture and intelligence enough to appreciate
the influence of comfort and beauty in the development of mind
and heart, must rejoice in the help which such appliances as
these, so artistically and tastefully arranged, will furnish for the
carrying on of the work of drawing out, improving and adorning
the mental faculties of those entrusted to their care.

I can speak with knowledge and with confidence of the deep solicitude with which these, my associates, have looked forward to this hour and to these services which assure us that the grand and holy purpose of these Trustees is completed. I can vouch for their gratitude; and I believe that, by this good work, they will be stimulated to devote their best efforts to fulfil the ultimate object of these generous givers, namely, the cultivation of immortal minds for usefulness and happiness.

In the name of the Public School Committee, in the name of the present and future generations of parents and children who are to reap the benefits of this god-like act, I thank these Trustees of the Long Wharf for what *they* have done; and I thank you, sir, and your associates of the City Council, for what *you* have done, *cheerfully* done, and for what you are still willing to do, for the blessed cause of Public Schools.

At this point, Governor Cozzens stated to the audience that the State Commissioner of Public Schools, Henry Rousmaniere, Esq., was present, a Newport boy, whom he well remembered in his school days, and he took great pleasure, in introducing him on this interesting occasion. Mr. Rousmaniere stepped forward and addressed the audience as follows:

*Ladies and Gentlemen :*

I am here, as a native of Newport, to express emotions which are as much yours as mine. I am here also, as a humble brother in the great brotherhood of educators, to utter a few words of congratulation upon the dedication of this noble temple. He, whose young heart deeply loved beauty in art and nature, has a right in manhood to confess his love. Standing in the midst of this attentive throng, and surrounded by this

27

beautiful scenery, my soul, growing warm under the sunshine of the recollections of schoolboy pleasures, almost melts itself into words as I speak.

It seems but yesterday that we were schoolboys together, wandering during holidays over fields or on the beach. We generally tried to excel in our studies. . If occasionally lazy, our teachers reminded us of the giants, all sons of Newport, whose manly voices were then echoing in yonder State House, or neighboring church. These appeals ran like a thrill of joy through our jaded nerves. You, my young friends, are addressed by the same stirring voices. The same bright examples of genius, married to learning, appeal to your desire for distinction. Listening to the traditions of your fathers, your ears may still catch the polished language and classic sentiments of a Hunter. The silence of the library is broken for you, by the sainted Channing, as he discourses in a strain so etherial as to lead good men to love the writer, though they do not sympathize with his theology; to listen to the preacher, though they do not embrace his doctrines.

You, my young friends, are admonished to do your duty in school, by the successful examples of many others, who were once, as you are now, humble scholars; but though their bodies sleep quietly under the earth, yet their fame will know no grave.

To-day, in your behalf, our mature minds send up blessings to the Almighty Giver of light and grace, for this school-edifice, so much more commodious than those which invited our schoolboy footsteps. To-day our heart of hearts rejoices that you are to receive, within these spacious rooms, literary instruction far more appropriate than that which partially moulded our young minds.

I conjure you, the pupils of these schools, in the hearing of

my voice, to achieve success in your studies. Lay down at
once a wise plan for the disposal of your leisure hours. Cling
to your books, as the greatest poet of Portugal clung to his epic
poem, clinching it between his teeth, as he swam from a sinking
ship, safely ashore. Perseverance will not always insure
wealth or happiness. But perseverance will create usefulness,
respectability, and power. Poverty may dog your steps. Lux-
ury may frown at you on the sidewalks. School Committees
may pronounce you stupid. Even your teacher, tired by your
perverseness, may lose all sympathy for you. Yet, remember
that he who has a strong will holds his destiny in his own
hands, either for good or ill. Sixty years ago, there was a lad
in Massachusetts who was denounced as a hopeless reprobate
by the School Committee, by the Trustees, and by several
teachers. At last there came a new teacher; he was advised
to turn this lad out of school. Even the father declared his
son was incorrigible. But the teacher had no little experience
in human nature; he treated the castaway firmly, but gently.
He complimented him the first day of the term; the lad looked
up astonished, for he feared a rough blow, instead of kind
words. It is not necessary to narrate particularly the steps of
this scholar from despair to hope, from a bad to a good reputation. Do you not know the name of this unpromising scholar?
It was the distinguished statesman of New York, William L.
Marcy,* so eminent as a Senator in Congress, so able a Secretary of State in James K. Polk's administration.

Begin, my young friends, now to build up in yourselves the
elements of a substantial character. Another generation of
youth shall be inspired by your deeds to work bravely, and
speak honestly, for their native State and beloved country.

---

* This gentleman was at one time a teacher in Eleazer Trevett's school, in
Newport.

Never make a promise to be broken; never learn a fact without ascertaining the cause of it. Never adopt a belief without argument. Never dislike a person without cultivating charity.

This, fellow citizens, is not a proper time to go into a minute investigation of the errors in plans of instruction. I shall allude to a few briefly. There is the old idea, not yet dead, that the mind, like a log of wood, can be chopped into any form. Such was the vagary of the Hindoos who made war on the instincts of human nature by their system of caste, thereby depriving individuals of happiness, and the nation of independence. The dreams of Plato for a state of perfection are sublime in theory, but absurd in practice. Lancaster foolishly fancied that he, by his flying artillery of monitors, could create genius, change nature, and install mere art as the deity of the school room. His scheme was a miserable abortion. Equally disastrous will all efforts be to level the distinctions of genius, and reduce the growth of immortal minds to a mere mechanical routine. There is too much routine even in the best plans. Too much homage is paid to the lifeless form of words, and too little to the living soul of thought. The mere memory is often honored with almost divine worship, while the analytic and creative faculties make but a few proselytes. Instruction is often levelled so as to render the higher faculties of children almost stagnant.

True education fills the memory with facts, infuses a larger life into the reason, and brims the moral affections with truth. Education aspires to lead men to think well and act nobly. How miserable that system of cramming which hurled Lord Byron upon a world which he hated, and which in return hated him. His passions were gorged, and his moral nature starved. He was like a ship on fire on an ocean of gunpowder.

What was the real value of the instruction which brought forth Edgar Poe in agony, and nursed him with food so bitter as to pervert his whole moral taste? His sensual passions sank him to a level with the brute, yet his imagination was so lofty that no modern eagle has scaled its dizzy height.

The main aim of education ought to be to elevate the moral affections, and thus promote the happiness of the race. The cultivation of the memory, or of any single faculty, cannot avail much. To achieve the desired result, knowledge must be perfumed with reason and baptized with conscience. Education ought also to pour showers of light on all the practical affairs of life. It ought to give dignity to labor and self-respect to the laborer. Knowledge must be taught to work in low positions without shame, and in high ones without vanity; or, in other words, nothing is low that is right, and nothing is high that is false. Education ought not only to cause two blades of grass to grow where but one grew before, but it ought to root the weeds of avarice out of public opinion, so that it would be a disgrace for one to grow rich by thrusting the roots of usury into the calamities of our country. Education ought to develop the individuality of each person, making his opinions his own as much as his face is his own. Men ought to be taught to think, not in mobs, not in masses, but singly, individually; for every man is an orb, revolving, not around other human orbs, but, around a great central sun, and that sun is eternity.

Education ought to prove that there is a law of progress in the human mind. The oracle of that progress is neither fashion, nor faction, nor self. The law of progress cannot be expounded by bigotry, nor analyzed by fanaticism. Progress has its home in minds that have fathomed their weaknesses, husbanded their strength, and know how (whether it is fashionable or unfashionable) to be magnanimous even to an enemy, charitable of others' motives, self-possessed in moments of general frenzy, and heroic at all times. So far as education does not seek to unfold the law of progress, it commits a grave error. Education can show that progress is never visionary nor presumptuous. What is new, if not practical, is of little value. The school house ought to be the vestibule of the structure of progress.

May all the institutions of learning in this city send every year into the community graduates grounded in every excellence. To physical beauty may they add moral loveliness; to grace of body may they unite flexibility and grace of mind. May these schools always be in practice, what they are designed to be be in theory, — the nurseries of good men and fair women; every hour being an advance toward virtue, justice, and patriotism. When those who are now teachers shall be removed to other stations, and those now scholars shall become teachers, may the change, in each instance, be an increase of happiness; and when you assemble in the High School in Heaven, where Jesus is the Teacher, may all look back to these schools as the first step in the revolution whereby hope began to bud into reality, knowledge blossom into faith, and time flower into eternity.

The Rev. William S. Child, Rector of Zion Church, then pronounced a benediction, when these deeply interesting services were brought to a close. The citizens were then invited to examine the different departments of the building, which elicited general satisfaction.

# APPENDIX A.

## HISTORICAL MEMORANDA.

*Historical reminiscences of Newport, which are alluded to in portions of this address, with others of interest, considered appropriate in this connection and worth preserving.*

The first newspaper printed in this State, was the Rhode Island Gazette, at Newport, in 1732; this was the fourth in New England. The first published in New York, was in 1733, Weekly Journal. The Newport Mercury, which is now in a more flourishing condition than ever, commenced June, 1758, and has been published ever since, excepting from December 2, 1776, to January 5, 1780, about three years, while the town was in the hands of the British, during which period it was suppressed.

In 1737, Newport contained seven churches, viz, one Episcopal, two Congregational, two Baptist, one Seventh Day Baptist, and one for Quakers.

In 1742, the most elegant and expensive mansion in New England, if not in America, was erected near Miantonomi Hill, on the spot now occupied by the residence of the family of the late J. Prescott Hall. It was built for, and occupied by, Godfrey Malbone, then doing an extensive business here; he was considered the wealthiest and principal merchant of those days on this continent. The house was destroyed by fire on the 17th June, 1766, during the preparation for a dinner party, to be given to a number of distinguished people, then on a visit to Newport. Mr. Malbone died in 1768.

In 1749, the clearances at the House of Customs on foreign voyages, were one hundred and sixty, and entries of arrivals, seventy-five.

1750. *October 20th.*—A remonstrance was sent from this town, passed in town meeting, to the General Assembly, against the proposed emission of paper money, stating that the town of Newport, the first and largest town in the colony, did not see any necessity for any such emission of bills, and in a most forcible, elaborate, and business-like document, portrayed its evil consequences ; this paper covers several pages on the town records of 1750, but is somewhat imperfect, in its being copied from the original record, which was sunk at Hurl Gate, near New York, alluded to elsewhere. It was really a very able document, and is well suited to the condition of our country even at the present time.

1753. It was estimated at this time that there were over three hundred sail of vessels, from sixty tons and upwards, owned in Newport.

1755. Newport contained 6,754 inhabitants, not including all doing business as seamen, who were absent at the time of taking the census. Providence contained 3,159.

1758. *August.*—To show the estimate that the General Assembly of the Colony placed upon Newport, it appears that they voted an appropriation of ten thousand pounds sterling towards building and fortifying Fort George, provided the town of Newport would vote five thousand more. The town meeting called for this purpose thought this very unreasonable, and appointed a committee to draw up an address, requiring the Assembly to appropriate more money, and show reason why Newport should be taxed so much.

1759. The Assembly ordered a State tax, in which Newport was assessed £2,200, and Providence £667. The members from Newport protested against the assessment as unequal, and further representing that the merchants of Newport had lost over two millions of money since the commencement of the present war—the French war.

1761. An account taken of the number of houses in Newport at this time, shows there were 888 dwellings, and 439 warehouses and other buildings.

1763. The Jewish Synagogue, on Touro Street, being finished, was dedicated this year on the 2d of December, to the God of Abraham, with great pomp and magnificence, according to the custom of the Hebrews. There were at this time over sixty families of Jews in Newport, among them many merchants of great wealth and enterprise.

1769. The first act of violence and resistance to the British authorities in America, took place at Newport this year, in the destruction of the sloop Liberty, one of His Majesty's armed vessels stationed here.

1771. The English armed vessels stationed and rendezvoused at Newport at this time, consisted of two frigates and nine ships of war.

1774. A census of the Colony this year. Whole number in the Colony 59,628, viz : 54,435 whites, 1,432 Indians, 3,761 negroes. Newport contained 9,209 ; Providence 4,321 ; this only included persons actually in the place at the time of taking the census. Seamen, of which so many belonged to Newport, and all others absent, were not taken into the account ; those added would have increased the population of the town to about 12 000.

Resolutions were sent this year to the town of Boston, in regard to the order of Parliament, to shut up their port, when it was done ; a town meeting was called, and it was voted to instruct our deputies to use their utmost influence at the approaching session of the General Assembly to procure and offer relief to the inhabitants of said town of Boston, making common cause with their sufferings.

1775. The harbor and bay of Newport were at this time occupied by a large number of vessels of war, which not only resorted here, as the most commodious and convenient, but most important naval station on the whole coast ; also with a view to a strict enforcement of the revenue laws at this then most important port of importation. In view of the great danger now being apprehended, large numbers of the inhabitants, including many of the principal merchants, removed from Newport, and established themselves in other and more inland places. •

1776. On the first of December, seventy sails of British men-of-war and transports arrived in Narragansett Bay, destined for Newport ; they came in by the west passage, around the north end of Conanicut, and during the week they landed eight or ten thousand men in Newport, or near by, at Middletown ; several regiments landed on this Long Wharf; this was by far the most serious affliction we ever experienced, remaining in Newport, and on the Island, as they did, long enough to destroy everything around them. During the operations of the hostile armies, a great part of the Island was rendered a scene of desolation ; all the houses situated between the two armies were burnt ; orchards full of fruit trees were cut down, wells filled up, and every damage that could be imagined was done, by order of the British Commander.

1779. On the morning of Monday October 25, while the British troops were preparing to evacuate the town, a proclamation was made, requiring the inhabitants to keep within their houses during the day, on pain of death for disobedience.

The French fleet that arrived here in July, proved a great acquisition ; at every movement they made, the officers of the British vessels became alarmed, and on one occasion three frigates and many other vessels were run on shore and fired ; others were sunk for the purpose of obstructing the channel.

The particulars connected with the removal of the army, and all their ord-

28

nance and stores, together with the condition of the town, is deeply interesting, and would make a chapter of itself. One of the most serious and wicked acts, was removing all the Town and Probate records, which were taken away in one of the transports. This act was ascribed to some of the Royalists who it was supposed intended to hold them for the purpose of making their peace at some future time. The vessel in which the records were shipped, was sunk in Hurl Gate near New York, by which accident they were nearly all destroyed, having laid a long time under water.

1780. The General Assembly met at Newport, for the first time after the evacuation of the Island, in September, and the session was held in the Redwood Library. The State House, having been ·used for barracks, and hospitals, was in shocking condition and needed repairs, etc.

This was the year also of the celebrated cold winter, for forty days ; the poor and suffering inhabitants who had escaped the dangers of war, experienced the greatest distress for fuel, which could not be had; the old buildings, wharf logs, and every other expedient was resorted to ; the Long Wharf, although previously destroyed to the water's edge, was this year stripped of everything in the shape of a log, that would burn, even though under water and very difficult to procure.

In 1782, the Town Council of Newport made application to Gen. Carlton, in command of New York, for the return of the Town records, which had been taken away at the evacuation of the town in 1779. In December they were returned under a flag of truce, with a polite letter from Gen. C., expressing his sorrow for the damage they had sustained by the sinking of the transport, and their having lain three years without examination. When received, they were in such a dilapidated condition that there was not energy enough in our people to attempt their restoration by re-copying ; occasionally they were resorted to, by some persevering; patient seeker for establishing a title, or proving a claim. It was not until December, 1857, the authorities deemed it an object to make a thorough re-copy of all that could be saved from the records of the Town Meetings, by which nearly one half has been rescued, and that only in part, as portions of almost every line, and of every page, are imperfect ; frequently five or ten pages together, perfectly unintelligible. The real estate and Probate records, consisting of over thirty large volumes, were so completely water-soaked, and rotted and matted together, that when opened, they crumbled to pieces, and not a single leaf could be made out perfect ; they are preserved in the record office in this shape, sickening to behold, and almost useless, so far as proving any title, or being of any service.

1784. A French squadron arrived here on the 22d September, and on the 24th October General Lafayette arrived as the guest of General Greene. This year·the General Assembly instructed their delegates in Congress to procure the consent of that body, to hold their next meeting at Newport, and offered to furnish suitable buildings. On the 26th May, Mr. Ellery, one of the delegates, moved that Congress adjourn to meet in Newport, on the 26th October. After some debate, Newport was stricken out, and Trenton, New Jersey, was substituted.

1785. One John Goodrich, senior, an American refugee, arrived in Newport soon after the peace, and asked liberty to settle here with his family, and become an inhabitant of the town, offering, in case permission was granted, to bring twenty sail of vessels which he owned, and establish himself in mercantile business; but as he had taken an active part during the war, in fitting out privateers, etc., the town voted, by a large majority, that he should not be allowed to settle in the place.

From 1775 to 1800 the newspapers contain a most wonderful amount of obituary, and biographical notices of the death of the early merchants of Newport; some of them of·a very interesting character, showing their position, the extent of their business, etc., and what is particularly noticeable, the large number·of them that *died* in other cities, and inland towns, whither they had retreated during the troublous days of the Revolution.

1798. *August* 21.—The frigate Constitution, Captain Barry, arrived at Newport. This is the identical old ironsides, that is now stationed opposite the end of Long Wharf, moored at Fort Wolcott, and used as one of the school ships of the Naval Academy, looking as young as she probably did on her first trip to Newport, sixty-five years ago—really she is a veteran.

1805. A new line of packet ships was started again, to ply between here and Charleston, South Carolina. From this time, also, there were many vessels engaged in the Russia trade. Their cargoes of iron were principally landed on the Long Wharf. Business generally seemed to be reviving, when it was sadly interrupted by the embargo of 1808. From this time, a general depression again came over our merchants, and for several years, they labored under great disadvantages. During these years, the Long Wharf was very much used. So many of the old wharves having been destroyed, this wharf, and the stores that had been built thereon, were very much in demand; but the continued decline from 1812 to 1832, offers but few incidents sufficiently important to notice in this connection. Since 1832, Newport has been improving again, having attracted men of wealth from the surrounding cities. They have been, and are purchasing lots, and building houses; and in time, we hope that they, or their children, will realize, in their adopted home, the advantages of our harbor and bay for commerce, and thus aid in restoring the commercial prosperity that Newport once enjoyed.

There are many very striking and interesting incidents in the history of these times, that would, no doubt, give great satisfaction to the readers of this Appendix. I have made a few selections which have a particular bearing upon the Long Wharf, and other points suggested in this address, hoping that some one may yet conceive the magnanimous idea of compiling and printing, in book form, the historic, chronological account of material occurrences, from the first settlement of Newport, collected and prepared by the late Hon. Henry Bull, which has been inserted, in small doses, in the venerable Newport Mercury, during the past few years, adding to it all matters of interest that might be gathered from other sources. There is enough to make a book that would be valued beyond calculation, and would serve to hand down to future generations the events of two hundred years, with its traditions, the character of the men who once lived, flourished, and died on this beautiful island. I commend this object to the attention of my fellow citizens, hoping it will be done, and well done.

# APPENDIX B.

Abraham Redwood, the founder and liberal patron of the Redwood Library, came from Antigua and settled in Newport early in the last century; he died March 8, 1788, at the age of 79 years.

Henry Collins, a distinguished merchant and native of Newport, was born in 1699. Possessed of great liberality and enterprise, he was at the head of every public improvement in Newport — the extension of the Long Wharf, the building of the Brick Market, &c., &c. His gift of the beautiful lot of land on which the Redwood Library was erected, in 1748, will more, perhaps, than any other of his liberal deeds, perpetuate his name and virtues through unnumbered generations. One hundred and fifteen years have already passed since that generous gift was made; the parchment deed of which has lately been framed, and suspended on the walls of the library. This library, now enlarged, renewed, and placed on a more substantial basis than ever before, may for hundreds of years to come continue to present, in ever living freshness, the name of its munificent benefactor. Mr. Collins died in 1770.

Abraham and Judah Touro, both sons of Isaac Touro, were born in Newport, Abraham in 1774, Judah in 1775; they were of the Jewish faith and order. Abraham became an eminent merchant of Boston, and at his death, in 1822, bequeathed liberal sums of money to keep in perpetual repair the Jewish Synagogue in Newport, and the street which bears his name. Judah established himself in New Orleans, became one of her heaviest merchants, and most munificent benefactors. At his death, in 1854, he, too, remembered the land of his birth, and the graves of his ancestors. The splendid fence around the Jewish cemetery was built at his expense, and he bequeathed ample means to keep it and the cemetery in repair forever. His bequest to the City of Newport, of ten thousand dollars, towards the purchase of the Stone Mill Lot, now Touro Park; also gifts to the Redwood Library, and an endowment to the Synagogue. These numerous instances of their benevolence and generosity will establish their lives and character beyond the rust of time, and while Newport lasts, their names will never be forgotten. Their remains were both brought to Newport, for interment in the Jewish cemetery on Touro Street.

Charles B. King, a native of Newport, born 1786, died in Washington, D. C., March, 1862, always retaining a strong affection for his birth place. His magnificent donations and bequests to the Redwood Library, in Newport, of all his books, his engravings and plates, with a gallery of upwards of two hundred pictures ; besides one-quarter of all the residuary interest in his estate ; yielding, as it will, nearly ten thousand dollars in cash, together with an equal interest in his residuary estates (ten thousand dollars more) to the Young Ladies' High School, in Newport ; are remembrances which history will ever perpetuate, when the marble tablet will be defaced and corroded by time, and the pure interest of affection shall have outlived itself.

# APPENDIX C.

## ABSTRACT

FROM THE

# RECORD OF THE LONG WHARF TRUSTEES,

PREPARED BY DAVID G. COOK, CHAIRMAN OF THE BOARD.

---

1795. *January.*—The first Record in the book of the doings of the Trustees of the Long Wharf, Hotel, and Public School, is a copy of the Act of the General Assembly, passed at the January session, 1795. It authorizes thirty-six persons, whose names are as follows: Henry Marchant, George Gibbs, George Champlin, Christopher Champlin, James Robinson, Peleg Clarke, Henry Sherburne, John Bours, Oliver Warner, John Handy, Francis Malbone, Daniel Mason, Ethan Clarke, Christopher Fowler, Simeon Martin, Thomas Dennis, John L. Boss, Samuel Vernon, Junior, Christopher Ellery, Christopher G. Champlin, William Ellery, Junior, Daniel Lyman, Isaac Senter, Benjamin Mason, Aaron Sheffield, William Littlefield, Silas Deane, Audley Clarke, Constant Taber, Caleb Gardner, Nathan Bebee, Moses Seixas, Nicholas Taylor, Walter Channing, Archibald Crary, and Robert Rogers, to set forth a scheme to raise by Lottery $25,000 for rebuilding the Long Wharf, in Newport, and for building a hotel; and they were authorized to appoint managers for said Lottery, and that they, or any eleven of them, were authorized to appropriate the money so raised, for the rebuilding of the Long Wharf, and hotel, and that the said thirty-six persons be appointed Trustees, for the management and direction of the said Long Wharf and hotel, and for receiving the rents and profits thereof, the net amount of which, after deducting the charges and repairs on the same, to be appropriated to the building and support of one or more public schools, for the use and benefit of the children in said town, in such manner as the said thirty-six Trustees may direct.

In case of vacancy by death, resignation, or otherwise, of any of the Trustees, the person or persons to succeed to such vacancy shall be chosen by a majority of votes of the surviving Trustees ; provided, that no such choice shall be made until the Trustees are reduced to a less number than twenty-one, which is always to be the number of Trustees.

1795. *February* 14.—At the first meeting of the Trustees, Henry Marchant was Chairman, and Moses Seixas, Secretary, five of the Trustees were appointed a Committee to report a scheme for a Lottery ; four others were appointed to inquire into the rights by which the Long Wharf is held, and in what manner a cession of the fee can be made to the Trustees. The Act of the Assembly was ordered to be published in the *Newport Mercury*, and the Trustees were to be notified to meet at Mr. Roger's Academy, the next Wednesday, at 6 P. M.

*February* 18.—Twenty-one Trustees met. *Voted*, That George Gibbs and George Champlin be appointed Managers, and that they give bond to the State, for the faithful performance of the Trust, and that they be reimbursed their expenses, and compensated for their services.

Moses Seixas was appointed Secretary to the Board of Trustees, and to be compensated for his services. It was *Voted*, That the quantum for compensation to the Managers of the Lottery, and Secretary, shall be determined by the Trustees.

William Marchant and Daniel Lyman were appointed to draft a Charter for the Incorporation of the Trustees.

The Committee to examine into the rights and title to the Long Wharf, to be continued, and as soon as they can ascertain the same, they are to consult with Mr. Marchant and Mr. Lyman as to the best mode of procuring the cession of the fee to be invested in the Trustees, and that they report the draft of cession, conveyance, and acts necessary, to the Trustees.

*Voted*, That a meeting of the Trustees be convened whenever the Secretary and Managers, either of the Committee, or eleven of the Trustees, may think proper.

1795. *Feb.* 25.—A committee was appointed to notify G. Gibbs and G. Champlin of their appointment as Managers of the Lottery, and to make report at the next meeting. The Secretary was directed to wait upon each person appointed by the Legislature to set forth a scheme for the Lottery, and those who have not met or acted, be requested to declare their acceptance or rejection of their appointment. The thanks of the Trustees were voted to Col. Robert Rogers, for the use of his academy.

*March 2.*—At at a meeting of the Trustees, the Committee reported that George Champlin and George Gibbs accept their appointment as Managers of the Lottery. Five others reject their appointment, and three more were absent, and were so previous to the meeting of the first Board.

*Sept. 9.*—At a meeting of the Trustees, G. Gibbs and G. Champlin having reported to the meeting that Simeon Potter, Esq. had, by Deed of Gift, made a donation of two lots of land, on Easton's Point in Newport, with a dwelling-house and store thereon, to be combined with the Fund to be established by the Newport Long Wharf and Public School Lottery, for the support of Public Schools in this town; it was therefore unanimously

*Voted and Resolved*, That G Gibbs and G. Champlin be requested to present the thanks of the Trustees to Simeon Potter, Esq. for his liberal donation, and to assure him that it shall be inviolably appropriated to the establishment and support of Public Schools, he has so generously patronized.

---

THE FOLLOWING IS A COPY OF MR. POTTER'S LETTER.

SWANSEY, May 16, 1795.

MESSRS. GEORGE GIBBS AND GEORGE CHAMPLIN:

*Gentlemen:* I saw in the *Boston Centinel*, a scheme of a Lottery, for the laudable intention of rebuilding the Long Wharf in Newport, the building a Hotel, and more especially establishing a Free School, which has determined me to make a free gift of my estate on the Point called Easton's Point, which came to me by way of mortgage, for a debt due from Hays and Pollock ; if you will accept of it in Trust to support a Free School forever, for the advantage of the poor children of every denomination, and to be under the same regulations as you desired the Free School should be that you design to erect. If you, gentlemen, will please to get a deed wrote agreeably to the intentions here manifested, I will sign and acknowledge the same, and send it to you for recording. I would only mention that if the situation is agreeable to you, the house and garden would do for a schoolmaster, and the oil

29

house, which is large, might be fitted up for the school house. This as you may think proper. There is no person here that understands writing such a deed, or I would have sent it to you completely executed.

I am, gentlemen, with respect,

Your very humble servant,<br>SIMEON POTTER.

————

*Voted*, That Thomas Dennis and John L. Boss, be requested to take charge of the house, store, and land, presented by Simeon Potter, to rent the same, and appropriate the rents to the repairs, in such manner as they may deem most advantageous.

*Voted*, That G. Champlin, J. Robinson, and D. Lyman, be requested to apply to the Society of Friends in this town, and solicit a relinquishment of the quitrent on said lots.

The Managers of the Lottery proposed to fix the drawing of the Lottery for the first Thursday of January next, which was agreed to by the Board.

1796. *Nov.* 20.—At a meeting of the Trustees, in consequence of several of the proprietors of the Long Wharf (east of Gravelly Point) having voluntarily offered, for themselves, and given encouragement that the whole of the proprietors would relinquish to the Trustees, for the public uses they were appointed for, all the right, title, and interest the present proprietors have in and to that part of the Long Wharf from the west side of Gravelly Point to the channel west of it, therefore, it is

*Voted and Resolved*, That, J. L. Boss and three others be appointed a Committee to apply to said proprietors for a cession of the same to this Trusteeship, to and for the public uses they were appointed for; and that upon such cession, with a legal title to that part of the wharf west of Gravelly Point, if the proprietors will stipulate to put and keep in good repair that part of the Long Wharf eastward of Gravelly Point, which shall be retained by them; that then the Trustees will, immediately after the opening of the spring, commence to rebuild the aforesaid part of the Long Wharf so ceded to them, and keep the same in good repair. The Committee are also to inform the said proprietors that unless a legal and absolute title or cession shall be made to the Trustees, they cannot undertake the rebuilding of the wharf. An immediate answer is required, in order that the Trustees may govern themselves accordingly.

Adjourned to Monday evening, 5th December.

*December* 5.—At the meeting, no quorum being present, no business was done.

The Committee observe, that from the number of unsettled acounts, it is impossible to ascertain what prizes have not been demanded within the time limited by the scheme ; but when their accounts are finally closed, the Lottery will be benefitted by the amount of all prizes which shall not have been paid by the managers, or persons who have sold shares and tickets on account of the Lottery.

The committee appointed to expend the rents of the school house in repairs, report that there is now due $118.33.

*Voted,* That all the rents that may be due for six months for the school house be expended in repairs, the balance to be paid from the funds of the Lottery.

A committee was appointed to report a plan for rebuilding the Long Wharf, and an estimate of the cost.

The proprietors of Easton's Point released and quitclaimed the two lots given by Simeon Potter from all demands for quitrent, by deed dated March 5, 1796, to the Trustees, called in the deed, " The Newport Incorporated School Committee."

1798. *March* 22.—At a meeting, the Committee to adjust the accounts of the Managers of the Lottery, made the following report :

That they have examined and adjusted said accounts and find
| | |
|---|---:|
| there is deposited in the Bank of Rhode Island, | $6,576 17 |
| Balance of accounts and notes deposited in said Bank for collection, | 5,973 97 |
| Making, | $12,550 14 |

There is no record of how much was realized from the accounts and notes above mentioned, out of which there will be a small deduction for charges on the sale of shares and tickets. They report that the Lottery, on the part of the Managers, has been conducted with the most perfect regularity and punctuality, and they have generously relinquished their commissions for their management, and they, in the opinion of the Committee, highly merit the thanks of the Trustees and the public.

The report was unanimously accepted and the substance ordered to be published in the *Newport Mercury,* with the thanks of the Trustees to Messrs. G. Gibbs and G. Champlin for their faithfulness in the management of the Lottery, and for their generosity in declining to accept any commission or compensation.

*Resolved*, That the moneys standing in the names of the Managers on the books of the bank be transferred to the credit of the Trustees at said bank.

The Committee are also directed to receive all notes and unsettled accounts of the Lottery, and to call for payment thereof, as soon as may be, and deposit the cash as collected in the Bank of Rhode Island, in the name of the Trustees.

*Resolved*, That Messrs. Gibbs and Champlin be discharged from their responsibility as Managers, and that application be made to the Legislature that the bonds given to the State be surrendered to them and cancelled.

*Resolved*, That the Committee appointed for obtaining the right and title to the lower part of the Long Wharf be instructed to apply to the Town Council for a meeting of the town to take into consideration the mode of transferring the right of the lower part of said Long Wharf to the Trustees, for the uses for which the money raised by Lottery is to be appropriated.

A Committee was appointed to prepare rules and regulations for the well ordering and government of the Trusteeship.

1799. *February* 23. The Committee appointed to report a plan for rebuilding the Long Wharf not having effected the purpose, S. Vernon and S. Dean were added to the Committee.

*April* 15.—*Resolved*, That the Committee advertise in the public papers for propositions for building the Long Wharf by contract, to state the manner in which it is to be built, the materials required, the depth of water, and every particular in detail; that they be authorized to divide the same into several contracts in such manner as will facilitate the undertaking, and when offers are received to lay them before the Trustees.

*July* 19.—*Resolved*, That J. L. Boss, S. Vernon, T. Dennis, C. Fowler and D. Lyman be a Committee to build the Long Wharf, and are authorized to make contracts and adopt such measures as are necessary to complete the same, keeping in view that they are not to exceed the amount of funds appropriated for that purpose, and that the said Committee be authorized to draw on the Treasurer for such sums as may be necessary for the completion of the Wharf.

Constant Taber was appointed Treasurer, and authorized to receive all moneys on account of the Institution, and to pay all drafts drawn by any three or more of the Committee, to build the Long Wharf. T. Dennis and J. L. Boss authorized to expend the rents received for the house on the Point in repairs, and settle their account with the Treasurer.

1800. *April* 28.—The Committee for building the Long Wharf were directed to proceed in completing said wharf, in such manner as they may

think proper, and that the money raised by the rent of the wharf, or lease
of lots adjoining the same, be pledged for defraying the expenses incurred in
finishing the wharf, in addition to the moneys heretofore appropriated for
that purpose.

*Resolved,* That the use of the building presented by Simeon Potter, Esq.
be tendered to the town for a school house, on condition of the town repairing the same, and paying such rent as may be agreed upon, provided it is
appropriated for a school, conformably to the act of the Assembly for establishing free schools, and that it be called the Public School.

1801. *May* 11.—At a meeting, the Committee to build the Long Wharf
represented that the funds were expended, and that a large sum of money
was yet required for completing the wharf; it was, therefore—

*Resolved,* That the Treasurer be authorized to borrow from the Bank of
Rhode Island, in addition to what is now due said bank, $1,800, at bank inter-
est, which sum is appropriated towards completing the wharf, to be paid on
the orders of the Committee.

*Voted,* That the Long Wharf, its rents, and profits, are hereby pledged to
the Bank of Rhode Island, as security for the payment of principal and
interest, of whatever may be due said bank. The Committee at the next
meeting to report a statement of the account and contract, and that they,
with G. Gibbs, G. Champlin, and Caleb Gardner, be a committee to examine
the state of said Long Wharf and to direct what is needful to be done, and
that they provide a plan for leasing the lots, and report to the next meeting
of the Board.

1802. *July* 19.—The propriety of the Trustees taking any shares in the
Company forming for carrying water down the Long Wharf was debated, and
unanimously determined in the negative. A committee was appointed to
procure a wharfinger. Thomas Dennis was authorized to sell at public
auction, after three weeks' notice, the materials which composed the building
to the eastward of the Potter House, and to have the lot fenced. A committee was authorized to examine the Long Wharf and to direct what is
needful to be done. They were also authorized to lease or sell the building
lots on the north side of Long Wharf belonging to the Institution, giving
them full power to do whatever appears to them proper in the premises.

*February* 26.—At a meeting, a committee was appointed to apply to the
Legislature to authorize the Treasurer to convey by deed, to the purchasers
of building lots on the north side of Long Wharf, all the title which the
Trustees have to the lots on the day of sale.

1805. *February* 13.—At a meeting a committee was appointed to audit the account of Jesse Barlow, wharfinger, and the said Committee were requested to devise a plan for making an addition to the south side of the wharf, with an estimate of the cost, and report to the next meeting, accompanied with a report of repairs, which the said wharf requires, and the cost.

*Resolved*, That Thomas Dennis be authorized to have the aqueduct water carried into the Potter House, and obtain from the tenants the best consideration he can for the convenience.

*Voted*, That Gibbs and Channing have permission to suspend the erection of any building on the easternmost lot on the Long Wharf, until they think proper, unless the Trustees should require it. Gibbs and Channing to lay a platform for landing goods, and to pay wharfage on goods for their own use, the same as if landed on the north side of their store ; they are not to make said lot a place of deposit, but are to remove the goods as soon as they conveniently can, other goods landed there to pay wharfage.

*August* 26.—At a meeting, the Committee to audit the account of Jesse Barlow, wharfinger, reported the sum of $439.76 due from said Barlow. It was *Voted*, That the Treasurer collect payment of said Barlow, also the balance of rent due on the Potter House.

Caleb Gardner was appointed Superintendent of Long Wharf, to make such repairs as he may deem necessary ; said Superintendent to appoint a wharfinger to be under his control.

*Resolved*, That yearly, and every year, the Trustees will meet on the second Monday of April for the transaction of business that may be necessary, the accounts of the past year to be exhibited, and the Superintendent to report what repairs and regulations may be necessary for the succeeding year. Rates of wharfage fixed, except that when whole cargoes are offered, circumstances may require a deduction therefrom.

1807. *June* 15.—A committee was appointed to audit the wharfinger's and Treasurer's accounts, G. Champlin was appointed Superintendent with the powers of the former Superintendent. Another committee was appointed to prepare a plan for widening the south side of the wharf, with an estimate of cost, etc. The Treasurer was directed to sue Jesse Barlow if he does not pay up the balance due.

*June* 29.—The Committee to audit accounts reported that the Treasurer's account shows a balance due the Bank of Rhode Island, 17 June, 1807, of $2,207.68, William Roberts' wharfinger's account shows a balance due from him of $186.18, for which he has given his note on demand. Thomas

Dennis's account of the Potter House shows a balance due him of $5.92. The Treasurer is directed to sign the account with the Bank of Rhode Island, showing the balance $2,207.68 as reported, to be due, also to sign the record.

The Superintendent was directed to require the wharfinger to settle his account, in future, on the first Monday in January, April, July, and October, to cause such regulations about fires on the wharf, and in stores, as may conduce to the general safety. All packets and coasters which lie at the wharf twelve hours, and whatever they may land or take off, shall be subject to wharfage, passengers' baggage excepted. The Secretary to make a list of Trustees, and that Simeon Martin call on each, and request those who accept the trust to write against their names, Accept, and those who decline will enter against their names, Resign, in order to know who serves, and that the vacancies be filled up, and report the same to the meeting to be held on Tuesday next, to which time this meeting is adjourned.

1807. *July* 8.—S. Martin reported that he had called on each of the Trustees; that nineteen Trustees accepted, but that John Bours, Archibald Crary, and Henry Shurburne had resigned. C. G. Champlin and G. Gibbs were elected Trustees to keep the number of twenty-one full. The Superintendent to have the Potter House painted, and he was authorized to adjust and settle the wharfage bill of ship Mount Hope on equitable terms. The question of widening the Long Wharf to be considered at the annual meeting.

· *Mem.* There is no record of meetings from July 8, 1807, to July 8, 1811. This was the period of the embargo, preceding the war of 1812.

1811. *July* 8.—At a meeting, Christopher Rhodes, William Engs, William Marchant, S. T. Northam, and Jonathan Bowen, were elected Trustees in the room of G. Champlin, F. Malbone, and Moses Seixas, deceased, and Daniel Lyman, and George Gibbs, removed out of town; William Engs was appointed Superintendent, and William Marchant, Secretary; R. Rogers to notify persons elected Trustees, and to obtain the signature of each declaring whether he accepts or resigns. Also to call on John Handy, Nicholas Taylor, C. G. Champlin, and William Littlefield, to know whether they are Trustees, and if so, to request their punctual attendance at meetings when notified. The meeting adjourned to Monday next.

*July* 15.—The Committee to examine accounts made a Report, that the balance due the Bank of Rhode Island was $1,274.01. The Treasurer was directed to certify the same. R. Rogers reported that he had called on the newly elected Trustees, who all accept; also on John Handy, and C. G. Champlin, who resign; also on Nicholas Taylor, and William Littlefield, who continue in the Trust. Robert Roberson, and Edward Martin were elected Trustees, in place of C. G. Champlin and John Handy, resigned.

William Engs appointed to take charge of the Potter House, and, with three others, as a committee, to call on the present occupants, and say to them that they must remove or pay the rent. R. Rogers and W. Marchant to examine into the claim against Jesse Barlow, and report to the Trustees. Another committee was appointed in relation to widening the wharf, eastward of the jog, and to report the probable expense thereof.

*July* 22.—At a meeting, the Committee on the claim of Jesse Barlow made their report. The Committee on widening the wharf eastward of the jog reported, and the subject was postponed.

*Mem.* No record of meetings from July 22, 1811, to August 14, 1814. This was also during the war. The wharf was used, but the energy to keep up the meetings was lacking.

1814. *August* 14.—At a meeting, a committee was appointed to examine accounts, and report at the next meeting, and, when prepared, to cause Trustees to be notified to meet.

*August* 19.—At a meeting convened by the Committee on accounts, they reported a balance due the Bank of Rhode Island, from Long Wharf, of $7.85. The account of William Engs was found correct, he being allowed 25 per cent on receipts. A committee was authorized to engage William Engs as Superintendent for the ensuing year. Gilbert Chace and John G. Whitehorne were elected Trustees, in place of James Robinson and William Marchant, resigned. R. Rogers was elected Secretary and Treasurer for the year. A committee was authorized to devise a plan for the commencement of a school, taking into consideration the present limited funds.

*August* 25.—The School Committee reported a plan for the commencement of a school for poor children as follows: Five Trustees to be appointed a School Committee, to rent the Potter House to a suitable person to keep a school, for such a number of boys belonging to families in the town who are unable to educate them; that they be instructed in reading, writing, and arithmetic, necessary for ordinary business and navigation; the Committee to superintend and adopt a code of rules for the government thereof, to be rigidly observed. As many boys admitted as the funds will support.

The Committee report that they have visited the Potter House, and find a room fifteen by forty feet with two fire-places, which, at small expense, can be converted into a good school room sufficiently large for fifty or sixty scholars, and the tenants, Joseph Finch and wife, who occupy the chambers keeping a school, who will undertake to instruct twenty or thirty children in reading, and find the necessary fire wood at $1.80 each, per quarter, a plan which the Committee recommend to be adopted for the ensuing winter, preparatory to enlarging the plan at the annual meeting, should the funds then admit. Job Gibbs, a carpenter who occupies the first floor, and is largely in arrears for rent, can be employed for making the necessary repairs for the accommodation of the pupils, on enlarging the establishment under the direction of an instructor in the higher branches.

J. L. Boss and four others were appointed a committee to carry the same into effect, and they are to have the sole charge of the Potter House, renting the same to the best advantage, to receive the rents either in tuition, labor, materials requisite for repairs, or money. The room for the school to be fitted up in such manner as they think proper. The Committee to make up quarterly accounts of expenses, and receipts for the house, tuition, books, and stationery ; are authorized to draw on the Treasury for the balance, and to make a report of the same to the annual meeting, or any other meeting of Trustees ; to keep a record of the pupils admitted, time of admission and dismission, books and stationery furnished. They are also authorized to call a meeting of the Trustees.

The Committee authorized to contract with William Engs, to continue Superintendent of the Long Wharf, are to engage him to remain until the annual meeting in April, except as to the Potter House.

*Resolved*, That the Secretary make out an account against Samuel Vernon for wharfage of brig Hannah, for six years at six cents per day, $131.46.

*August* 29.—The Committee before mentioned, reported that they had agreed with Capt. Benjamin Cozzens, as Wharfinger and Superintendent of Repairs, he to receive twenty-five per cent of receipts, and to have liberty to resign in case of peace between Great Britain and the United States.

1815. *January* 26.—Capt. B. Cozzens having gone to sea, the Committee were authorized to procure another wharfinger.

*April* 10.—The Committee are to direct all claims for wharfage to be put in suit by the Secretary.

W. Ennis, B. Hadwen, J. R. Sherman, and W. C. Gardner, were elected Trustees in place of C. Rhodes, W. Ellery, T. Dennis, and W. Engs, resigned.

*Resolved*, That the school be extended to a number not exceeding forty, at the discretion of the Committee ; notice to be given in both newspapers.

30

1815. *May* 1.—The Committee appointed August 14, reported that all the moneys advanced by Bank of Rhode Island for the wharf, were reimbursed, except $7.50.

A committee was appointed to devise a plan for commencing a school agreeably to the original intention of the grant, of the General Assembly. Owing to the limited funds arising from wharfage, it was deemed advisable to commence a school with a small number of boys, in the house presented for that purpose by Simeon Potter; a contract was accordingly made with Elizabeth Finch, who tenants a part of the house, and on the 10th October, 1814, school commenced, consisting of twenty-five small boys, who, on examination by the School Committee from time to time, and more particularly at the expiration of the second quarter, were found to have made greater progress in their learning than was anticipated, and that Mrs. Finch, with the assistance of her husband, had done ample justice to the pupils.

At the annual meeting, April 10th, the Committee were directed to enlarge the school to the number of forty, from a belief that the probable increase of the funds would authorize such augmentation; and measures were put in train to carry said resolve into effect, by obtaining pupils from different parts of the town, that' all may have an opportunity of experiencing the happy effect of so valuable an institution. The Trustees flatter themselves that the next annual report will not only be gratifying, but highly satisfactory, to all who feel an interest in promoting the welfare of the poor and necessitous.

*July* 10.—The Committee who had the matter in hand were authorized to settle with Mr. Vernon, by reference. William Hunter was elected a Trustee in place of Walter Channing, resigned.

*October* 10.—The report of the School Committee was received and approved. Samuel Vernon and John L. Boss were appointed a Committee to superintend the repairs requisite for the wharf (which has been materially damaged by the late disastrous storm of September 23, 1815), which they are requested to attend to without delay; and they are authorized to take up money on loan at the R. I. Union Bank, and Bank of Rhode Island, on such terms as may be agreed upon.

*October* 27.—*Resolved*, That, the Treasurer is hereby directed to sign a note or notes at such banks where the Committee appointed on the 10th inst. shall obtain loans of money sufficient for the repairs directed by said vote, and that the Long Wharf and the funds arising therefrom be and are hereby pledged for the payment of said notes.

The undersigned agree, as of a special meeting of the Trustees, that tho

Secretary enter on the records the above vote, as if done and passed at the meeting of the 10th October, 1815.

John L. Boss, William Ennis, Jonathan Bowen, Constant Taber, Simeon Martin, Silas Dean, Christopher Fowler, Stephen T. Northam, Robert Robinson, Gilbert Chace, Robert Rogers.

1815.  *September* 23.—The following account of the gale of September 23d, is from the *Newport Mercury:*

### AWFUL AND DESTRUCTIVE STORM.

On Saturday last, 23d inst., this town was visited by one of the most awful and destructive storms ever experienced here, sweeping away and laying prostrate almost everything in its course.  The gale commenced early in the morning at north east and continued increasing in violence (the wind varying from N. E. to S. E. and S. W.) until 11 A. M., when it began to abate, and about one o'clock all danger from the wind and tide was over and the afternoon was fair and mild, forming a striking contrast with the war of the elements which had existed but a few minutes before.  The tide rose three and a half feet higher than it had ever been known before.  At Providence it rose seven feet higher than ever before.

To attempt to particularize the suffering, to estimate the losses, is impossible.  Two dwelling houses and nine stores and workshops on the Long Wharf were carried away by the violence of the wind and tide, and those that withstood the gale are rendered almost untenable by the vessels, lumber, &c. being driven against them.  Several of the stores carried away contained a considerable amount of property in West India and other goods, which was nearly all lost.  One of the houses swept from the Long Wharf was occupied by Mr. Andrew V. Allan, and such was the rapidity and violence of the storm that every attempt to save his family was in vain; they all perished, his wife, three children and a girl that lived with them.

The wharves on the Point, with most of the stores, stables, &c., on them were carried away.  The wharves in other parts of the town, with the stores on them, also sustained very considerable injury, and everything movable on the wharves was swept away.  In some of the stores the water was four feet deep.  The Long Wharf has sustained great damage and the stores on the head of the wharf are much shattered, and their contents (flour, sugar, corn, tobacco, &c.) damaged by the tide.  The large three-story store of Gov. Martin was removed nearly six feet from its foundation.  A large three-story store on Rhodes & Cahoone's Wharf, containing hemp and flour, was taken from its foundation and floated into the harbor.

The town, after the gale, was a scene which defies description. Many of our streets were rendered impassable by the quantity of goods, lumber, wood, spars, wrecks of houses, vessels, trees, &c., lying in every direction. The steeples of the first and second Congregational Churches were partly blown down, the roofs of the Episcopal Church and First Congregational were partly carried away, and other public edifices have sustained considerable injury. We dare not venture to risk a calculation as to the amount of damage sustained, but it is very great. Many poor families have lost their all and were happy to escape with their lives. The scene was such as was never before witnessed by our oldest inhabitants. The uprooting of huge trees, some of which had braved the fury of the elements for nearly a century, part of the town inundated; the wind blowing a hurricane, a prodigious swell running, some buildings falling to pieces, the sea beating against others with a fury surpassed only by the breakers of our sea shore; and amidst all these horrors were seen families struggling to escape from their houses, and persons striving to save their property. After the storm the outside of the windows in the town was found coated with a fine salt which, it seems, was conveyed from the ocean through the air, and the leaves of the trees, from this cause, as is supposed, are curled and crisped as with a general blast.

Two brigs were driven on the tops of the wharves; four sloops were driven on the top of the Long Wharf; a sloop with wood was carried over the Long Wharf on to the Point; another was driven into the cove, and two sloops were sunk at Long Wharf. Much damage was done to the towns situated on the Narragansett Bay and along the shores, and a number of lives were lost in this disastrous gale.

1816. *January* 8.—At a meeting, a committee was appointed to report a plan for widening the wharf, with an estimate of the expense. Benjamin Hadwen was appointed Wharfinger.

*April* 8.—The Treasurer was ordered to put the demands against Thomas Dennis and S. Vernon in suit unless adjusted before 25th April. W. Ennis and W. C. Gardner to be a committee to audit the Treasurer's accounts.

*July* 8.—*Resolved*, That all vessels lying at the Long Wharf six hours be subject to one day's wharfage. A committee was appointed to revise the rates of wharfage and to report to the Wharfinger; the same to be adopted by him until the next quarterly meeting of the Trustees.

*October* 11.—Lewis Rousmaniere was elected a Trustee. The Wharfinger to put in suit all accounts due and unpaid.

1817. *April* 21.—At the annual meeting the Committee on the rates of wharfage made their report of rates to be charged, which was adopted, except that all vessels taking a berth, or fastening to a post, six hours to pay a day's wharfage, altered to twelve hours.

*Voted,* That a committee be appointed to audit the Treasurer's accounts.

1818. *January* 12.—*Resolved,* That the Treasurer be authorized to obtain a loan of $400 at either of the banks. A committee was appointed to settle all accounts against the Long Wharf and to draw on the Treasurer for the balance due.

*Resolved,* That the school be reduced to the number of ten scholars, to be selected by draft from the whole number. A committee was appointed to revise the rates of wharfage.

*July* 13.—A committee was appointed to settle the accounts of the Wharfinger.

1819. *January* 15.—A committee was appointed to settle with S. T. Northam for damage to a scow. The Committee on Wharfage made a report which was accepted; that the deduction allowed on landing cargoes or parts of cargoes be repealed, and that, on landing whole cargoes, ten per cent be allowed. Wharfinger to remove vessels not engaged in discharging or loading.

*April* 12.—At the annual meeting, *Resolved,* That the Wharfinger shall receive 25 per cent on receipts up to $200, over $200, 20 per cent.

A committee appointed on the question of building an addition to the wharf. A committee to superintend the school was elected for the year. A committee to superintend the wharf was elected. Benjamin Hadwen was elected Wharfinger. A report from the School Committee was received.

*July* 12.—A report of the School Instructors was referred to the School Committee, who were directed to inquire into the causes of the absence of those who are reported as delinquents, and to dismiss at their discretion, and have their places supplied with such as will be more punctual. The Committee on building an addition to the wharf were discharged from any further consideration of the subject.

*October* 11.—George Engs was elected a Trustee in place of Simeon Martin, resigned. S. Fowler Gardner was elected in place of Silas Dean, deceased.

William Hunter was appointed one of the School Committee in place of S. Dean, deceased.

1820. *January* 10.—J. L. Boss was appointed to take charge of Long Wharf, in place of B. Hadwen, wharfinger, during his sickness. J. L. Boss to receive terms and report an estimate of cost of repairing Long Wharf and the ways and means to carry the same into effect. Stephen Gould was elected Trustee, in place of Gilbert Chace, deceased. J. R. Sherman and G. Engs to audit Treasurer's accounts. The School Committee to notify Job Gibbs to settle the rent due, or leave before 1st April.

*January* 24.—John L. Boss was authorized to make a contract with Durfee and Friend for repairing the wharf on the best terms he can.

*Resolved*, That the Treasurer's account be audited annually, or oftener ; all moneys to be deposited in bank and no payments to be made except by checks ; and that the cashier cause the name of every person paid to be entered on the book, said bank-book to be balanced quarterly and the Treasurer to balance his account quarterly ; the Treasurer to be allowed $10 annually for his services.

*July* 10.—A committee was appointed to audit and settle the accounts of the Treasurer and Wharfinger. J. L. Boss and J. Bowen were appointed a Committee to contract for repairs of Long Wharf. Samuel Whitehorne was elected a Trustee, in place of L. Rousmaniere, deceased.

*April* 10. — At the annual meeting the Treasurer was authorized to obtain a loan of $50 at either bank. That from this date the Wharfinger shall be allowed 15 per cent on wharfage collected. Robert Rogers was elected Secretary and Treasurer for the year ensuing. A committee to superintend the school for the year was elected. A committee to superintend the wharf, and B. Hadwen, Wharfinger, were elected. A report of the instructors of the school was received and the balance due Joseph Finch directed to be paid by the Treasurer.

1821. *January* 8. — Benjamin Pierce was elected a Trustee, in place of S. Whitehorne, who declined. James Stevens was elected a Trustee, in place of John R. Sherman, resigned. ·

*April* 9. — Annual meeting. The Wharfinger directed to make a statement at every quarterly meeting of all sums due from persons or vessels for wharfage. R. Rogers re-elected Secretary and Treasurer. A new school committee chosen and B. Hadwen elected Wharfinger. A committee was elected to superintend the wharf.

*July* 9. — The Wharfinger was authorized to employ R. K. Randolph, as attorney, to attend to suits brought against R. Potter, and others, for wharfage.

1822. *January* 7. — Nathaniel S. Ruggles was elected a Trustee, in place of Edward Martin, resigned. Edward W. Lawton was elected a Trustee, in place of W. C. Gardner, resigned.

*April* 8. — Annual meeting. R. Rogers re-elected Secretary and Treasurer and B. Hadwen, Wharfinger. A school committee and a committee to superintend Long Wharf were appointed.

*October* 7. — Committee to superintend Long Wharf authorized to make necessary repairs. A committee was appointed to ascertain the best mode of repairing the wharf, to make it more convenient for small vessels to discharge, and to report the expense.

1823. *January* 13. — The Committee on repairing the wharf was continued and directed to report at the annual meeting. The account of Benedict Dayton was referred to Committee superintending the Wharf.

*April* 14. — R. Rogers re-elected Secretary and Treasurer. A school committee of five appointed for the year ensuing. Robert Stevens, Jr. was elected Wharfinger ; his commission to be 15 per cent. The Committee to superintend the wharf were re-elected.

1823. *July* 14.—The Committee for repairing the wharf, were discharged. J. L. Boss and G. Engs, were appointed a Committee to repair the school house. Robt. Stevens, Jr. was elected a Trustee, in place of Benjamin Pierce deceased.

*October* 13.—R. Rogers was added to the Committee for repairing the school house. The Wharfinger to adjust the account against owners of brig Brutus.

1824. *January* 12.—Treasurer directed to pay interest and $20 principal on notes at Bank, and renew said notes.

*October* 11.—David King was elected a Trustee, in place of J. L. Boss, deceased. R. Rogers re-elected Secretary and Treasurer, and Robert Stevens, Jr., Wharfinger. A School Committee was elected, and a Committee to superintend the wharf and to make such repairs as may be necessary.

1825. *April* 11.—Annual meeting, W. Ennis and G. Engs were appointed Auditors. R. Rogers was re-elected Secretary and Treasurer, and the School Committee were re-elected. A committee including R. Stevens, Jr., was appointed to superintend the wharf and to make such repairs as may be necessary, for the preservation of the same.

*October* 10.—A Committee was appointed to fix the rates of wharfage, and to advise with wharfinger.

1826. *April* 10.—Russell Coggeshall was elected Trustee, in place of John G. Whitehorne resigned. Nicholas G. Boss was elected a Trustee, in place of William Hunter, removed from town. R. Rogers was re-elected Secretary and Treasurer. Robert Stevens, Jr., was elected wharfinger. A School Committee and a Committee to superintend the wharf, were appointed.

1827. *February* 15.—At a meeting, S. T. Northam, Moderator, and George Engs, Secretary *pro tempore*, a Special Messenger was appointed to wait on the Secretary and request his attendance with the books. Mr. Engs reported that he could not find him ; wherefore it was

*Voted*, That, whereas by the last Will of Constant Taber, he has bequeathed to the Long Wharf Free School, a certain sum of money, it therefore becomes our duty to recover and receive said legacy ; that S. T. Northam and N. G. Boss, be a Committee to engage to support the interest of this Board in any legal contest.

*Voted*, That, the Chairman address a note to Mr. Rogers to call a meeting of the Trustees to-morrow at 11 o'clock, A. M.

*February* 16.—The meeting assembled at the call of Mr. Rogers, Secretary, at the time appointed. It was stated, that whereas constant Taber by his last Will, bequeathed to the Trustees of the Long Wharf, for the benefit of the Public School, thirty shares of U. S. Bank Stock, which legacy is annulled by a codicil, executed in March, 1826, and which codicil is contested as being illegally executed ; the Trustees deem it their duty to prevent the right of the Long Wharf Free School from being infringed. A Committee was appointed to attend the Court of Probate on Tuesday next, to employ counsel if necessary, and take such steps as may be proper, and report to the next annual meeting. It resulted in the employment of Mr. Randolph as counsel and the payment to him, for his services, of the sum of $60. Nothing was recovered under the will. Mr. Rogers entered on the Record a declaration that he was not applied to to issue a notice or call for a meeting, and was not to blame in the matter.

*April* 9.—Annual meeting. Richard K. Randolph was elected a Trustee, in place of Constant Taber, deceased. A School Committee and two Auditors were elected. R. Rogers was re-elected Secretary and Treasurer, and Robert Stevens, Jr. Wharfinger. A committee to superintend the wharf was elected.

*April* 12.—David M. Coggeshall was elected a Trustee, in place of Richard K. Randolph, who declines. A committee was appointed to revise the rates of wharfage. R. K. Randolph's account for services $60, ordered to be paid. A Committee of Observation was appointed in relation to C. Taber's Will. W. Ennis was appointed to apply to the General Assembly for an act regulating the Long Wharf, in removing vessels, &c.

*July* 27.—At a special meeting, the rates of wharfage reported by the Committee were adopted, and one hundred copies ordered to be printed. A committee was appointed to petition the Legislature for an Act authorizing the wharfinger to remove vessels whenever he may think proper. A committee was appointed to ascertain the expense of clearing both sides of the wharf from stone and gravel, and to have the same done without delay, at an expense not over $200.

1828. *April* 14.—Annual meeting. James Phillips was elected a Trustee in place of James Stevens, absent from the State. Auditors and School Committee re-elected. R. Rogers, Secretary and Treasurer, and R. Stevens, Jr., Wharfinger, re-elected. A committee to superintend the wharf and to make repairs, was appointed, also to repair the fence of School House Lot. Treasurer authorized to hire from either bank, any sum not over $200, at the discretion of the Committee, to have the stone and gravel cleared from the sides of the wharf.

1829. *April* 13 —Annual Meeting. Henry Bull was elected in place of Nicholas Taylor, Trustee, deceased. Thomas Bush, in place of Robert Robinson, Stephen Bowen, in place of Jonathan Bowen, John Stevens, in place of Stephen Gould, removed from town, were severally elected Trustees. Auditors and School Committee were appointed. R. Rogers, Secretary and Treasurer, and R. Stevens, Jr., Wharfinger, were re-elected.

*Voted,* That Mrs. Finch, widow of Joseph Finch, shall continue in the house, of which the rent is to be paid in schooling small children of both sexes, under the superintendency of School Committee.

A committee was appointed to settle with Newport Bank, and if requisite, to hire money of either of the other banks, to pay the Newport Bank. A committee was appointed to apply to the General Assembly for more extensive powers, in relation to Long Wharf. A committee was appointed to superintend the Long Wharf, and make necessary repairs. Another committee was appointed to call on the proprietors of the upper part of the wharf, respecting repairing the same, and also to lay the subject before the town at the next Town Meeting. The Secretary to furnish the Chairman of each

31

Committee, with a copy of the votes, specifying their appointment, and the business to which they are to attend.

*July* 13.—At a quarterly meeting, *Voted*, That the School Committee make an arrangement with the widow Dennis for schooling small children, for the rent of the house belonging to the Trusteeship.

H. Bull and J. Phillips were authorized to make a contract with the proprietors of the steam packets, for the use of the head of the Long Wharf, in conformity to the Act of the Assembly, May session, 1829, and were authorized to make such additions or repairs, as are required by the steamboats, or as they may think advisable, for the interest of said wharf. George Bowen was elected a Trustee in place of Stephen Bowen, deceased.

1830. *April* 12.—Annual meeting. The School Committee were again empowered to contract with Mrs. Dennis, or some other person, for the rent of the house, to be paid in schooling small children, under the direction of the Committee,—the Committee appointed for the year. A committee was appointed to superintend and repair the wharf.

The Committee appointed to call on the proprietors of the upper part of the wharf, respecting repairing the same, were requested to urge the propriety of its being done. The Superintending Committee to adjust the unsettled account of the steamer Chancellor Livingston as they may think proper. R. Rogers elected Secretary and Treasurer for the year, to receive $20 annual compensation. R. Stevens, Junior, was elected Wharfinger. Samuel Allen was elected a Trustee, in place of Christopher Fowler, deceased.

*July* 12.—At a meeting, the Superintending Committee were directed to continue the repairs on the wharf, as far as requisite, for the interest of the Trust; the Treasurer to hire at R. I. Union Bank a sum not exceeding $600, as may be required by the Committee to pay the bills.

1831. *April* 11.—At the annual meeting, Richard K. Randolph was elected a Trustee in place of Russell Coggeshall, resigned. Henry Bull resigned, and Isaiah Crooker was elected a Trustee in his place.

*Voted*, That David M. Coggeshall's account for $60, for superintending repairs, be allowed and paid by the Treasurer, and that $30 be paid to James B. Phillips for services in superintending repairs.

A school committee was elected and directed to rent a house for schooling children. D. M. Coggeshall was appointed Superintendent of repairs on Wharf and School House. A committee of vigilance was appointed to press the proprietors or Town Committee to complete the repairs on the road leading down the Long Wharf. R. Rogers was re-elected Secretary and Treasurer, and G. Engs and G. Bowen, Auditors. R. Stevens, Jr. was elected Wharfinger, to use all diligence in collecting balances due from steamer Chancellor Livingston and settle on the best terms he can.

*July* 11. — At a meeting, the Treasurer was authorized to borrow a sum not exceeding $140, to pay off the demands against the wharf. The Superintendent to advise with Audley Clarke, Moderator, respecting further repairs on the wharf.

*October* 11. — The Treasurer reported that bills amounting to $797.87, approved by the Superintending Committee, were all paid; that the Board is indebted to R. I. Union Bank, by note, $1050, the interest paid to 1st January, 1831, and that there is a balance in the Treasury of $42.82.

1832. *April* 9. — Annual Meeting. *Voted*, That the school under the care of Mrs. Dennis be discontinued, and that the house deeded by Simeon Potter to the Trustees be rented, and the rent appropriated to the repairs of said house, and that George Bowen is appointed to carry the same into effect.

*Voted*, That the bill of David M. Coggeshall of $30, for superintending repairs, be allowed and the Treasurer is directed to pay the same.

R. Rogers re-elected Secretary and Treasurer and the Auditors re-chosen for the year. Treasurer to examine and report at the next quarterly meeting the sums collected and balances due.

*Voted*, That the Wharfinger be allowed eight per cent on all sums collected from steamboats, and twenty per cent on all wharfage from other sources; and that it shall be the duty of the Wharfinger to superintend the common and necessary repairs for the preservation of the wharf, and that in his account he shall specify the articles and persons from whom he collects wharfage. Theophilus Topham was appointed Wharfinger in place of Robert Stevens, declined. George C. Mason was elected a Trustee in place of William Ennis, deceased.

1833. *April* 8. — Annual Meeting. R. Rogers was re-elected Secretary and Treasurer, and Theophilus Topham was appointed Wharfinger. Auditors were re-appointed. George Bowen was appointed to rent the Potter House, and pay the same into the Treasury. A committee was appointed to make an estimate of the expense of extending the south wall eighty feet and to advertise for proposals for doing the same. John V. Hammett was elected a Trustee in place of James B. Phillips, deceased.

*June* 3. — The committee in relation to extending the south wall reported verbally, that they had received proposals from William Vars, which were submitted, and it was

*Resolved*, That a committee of three be authorized to contract with William Vars to widen the Long Wharf one hundred feet in length, extending from the jog, on the terms proposed, and not exceeding the sum named ; that the said work be done under the inspection of said committee.

*Resolved*, That the Treasurer be empowered to hire money for carrying into effect the foregoing Resolution, on such terms as the committee shall direct, and that the Long Wharf and the funds arising therefrom be, and are hereby, pledged for the payment of the money borrowed.

That G. Engs and the Wharfinger be authorized to procure suitable ladders to reach to the ridge of the stores, to be kept in readiness on said wharf in case of fire ; also to procure twelve good buckets for the wharf, and to have the roofs of said stores whitewashed, as may be necessary, to guard against fire, consulting the owners on the expediency of the measure and whether they would join in defraying the expense.

*Resolved*, That G. Engs and G. Bowen be a committee to sell the house presented to the Trustees by the late Simeon Potter at such time and in such manner as they may think most advisable.

1834.  *April 7.* — Annual meeting.  R. Rogers, Secretary and Treasurer, and T. Topham, Wharfinger, re-elected.  Auditors re-elected.  Treasurer to notify them to audit his accounts for the past two years.  G. Engs and G. Bowen authorized to sell the Potter house, and if not sold, to let the same ; also to collect the back rents due.  Thomas Bush to have the bad places on the wharf levelled and filled up, expense not to exceed $25.  The Wharfinger directed in future not to collect wharfage on baggage, or carriages and horses of passengers, or on baskets of fruits and furniture brought for family use and not for sale.

*April 22.* — The committee authorized to sell the Simeon Potter house reported that they had sold the same at auction, previously advertised, to George Tilley, the highest bidder, for the sum of $505, payable in a note at ninety days, wherefore, it was

*Voted*, That Robert Rogers be authorized to convey to the said George Tilley all the right of the Trustees to the said lot and buildings thereon for the sum of $505.

A committee was appointed to dispose of the money received for the sale of house and lot.  Treasurer to pay expenses of sale and to pay the bill of Narragansett Bay Company.

*July 14.* — The committee on disposal of the proceeds of house and lot reported and recommended the money to be placed in Savings Bank on interest. Report received and the Treasurer directed to deposit the money in Savings Bank. A committee appointed to procure a portable gangway for landing passengers, &c. Thomas Bush authorized to draw on the Treasury for a sum sufficient to complete the repairs.

1835. *April* 13. — Annual meeting. Secretary and Treasurer, Wharfinger and Auditors re-elected. Thomas Bush a committee to complete the repairs already commenced. Stephen A. Robinson was elected a Trustee in place of Samuel Vernon, deceased.

*September* 14. — George C. Mason was elected Secretary and Treasurer in place of Robert Rogers, deceased. G. Bowen and John Stevens a committee to receive books and papers from the administrator of Robert Rogers, late Secretary and Treasurer, and deliver them to George C. Mason. Robert P. Lee was elected a Trustee in place of Robert Rogers, deceased. A committee was appointed to examine and report what repairs are necessary for the Long Wharf.

1836. *April* 12. — Annual meeting. George C. Mason was elected Secretary and Treasurer. Theophilus Topham, Wharfinger. G. Engs and G. Bowen, Auditors were re-elected. A committee of six were appointed to examine and report what repairs are required, and whether it is advisable to make any addition to the wharf; also to call on the captains of the steamboats and request them to be more careful of fire than heretofore while at the Long Wharf.

*July* 11. — A committee was appointed to place a chain across the head of the wharf to prevent passengers from being incommoded by hacks.

*September* 30. — A committee was appointed to confer with Mr. George Curtis, relative to a letter addressed by him to the Treasurer, in regard to Long Wharf. The Treasurer was directed to place the money on hand at the end of the quarter in Savings Bank.

1837. *January* 10. — At a meeting, Samuel Barker, Benjamin Finch and William Sherman were elected Trustees in place of Benjamin Hadwen, David King and N. G. Boss, deceased. Treasurer to place funds on hand in Savings Bank, provided said Bank will allow interest on the same.

*April* 11. — Annual meeting. G. C. Mason was elected Secretary and Treasurer, and Theophilus Topham, Wharfinger; G. Engs and G. Bowen, Auditors; T. Bush, J. Stevens and G. Bowen, a committee to examine wharf and make such repairs as are absolutely necessary.

*July* 17. — *Voted*, That the Wharfinger put so much gravel on the wharf as is absolutely required.   Theophilus Topham to be allowed $30 for services as Superintendent of Repairs on Wharf.

*September* 4. — The Wharfinger directed to prohibit all drivers of carriages, drays, &c., from going to the westward of the chain across the wharf while steamboats are landing or taking off passengers, and a committee was appointed to assist him.

1838.  *January* 9. — No quorum present.

*April* 9. — Annual meeting.   George C. Mason was elected Secretary and Treasurer and T. Topham, Wharfinger ; S. Barker and G. Bowen, Auditors. The Treasurer was directed to place the funds in his hands in Savings Bank, if interest is allowed.

*July* 10. — The Secretary was directed to furnish a copy of the Charter of this Corporation to the committee appointed by the town, to report upon the expediency of building a new Public School House.   George Bowen, a committee to make an estimate of the cost of building a new wall on the south side and west end of the wharf, and that he draw upon the Treasurer for such money as shall be necessary.

*October* 8. — G. Bowen and S. F. Gardner were appointed a committee to apply to the Town Clerk for the loan of the Report of the School Committee, made to the Town of Newport at a town meeting held October 6, 1838. The Treasurer was ordered to place in Savings Bank $500, if the Bank allows interest.

1839.  *January* 8. — *Voted*, That H. Bull's bill for railing, &c., on stores be paid.   A committee to purchase twelve leather buckets was appointed.

*April* 8. — George C. Mason, Secretary and Treasurer, and T. Topham, Wharfinger, re-elected.   Auditors re-appointed and a committee on repairs of the wharf appointed.

*July* 8. — No quorum.   G. Engs reported that the steamboats having left the wharf, the committee appointed do not deem it necessary to make any other repairs but such as the Wharfinger is authorized to make.

1840.  *April* 13. — Annual meeting.   The Secretary and Treasurer and Wharfinger re-elected ; Auditors re-appointed.

*Voted*, That all steamers coming to or going from Long Wharf shall shut their dampers, or so regulate their fires, as to prevent the fire issuing from the chimneys while the boat is within a cable's length, or one hundred and twenty fathoms of the wharf, and that a copy of this vote be forwarded to the

President of the New Jersey Steamboat Company, and also to each of the masters of the steamboats; and the Superintendent is directed to report any breach of said rule.

*July* 13. — *Voted*, That the Treasurer pay D. M. Coggeshall's bill, $12.16, and Finch and Engs', $35.43.

*Voted*, That $100 be given to the proprietors of the stores on the wharf towards the expense of plastering on the roofs, under shingles, provided the whole can be done. At this time all steamboats were using pine wood for fuel, and the sparks blowing on the roofs frequently set them on fire.

·1841. *April* 15. — Annual meeting. G. C. Mason, Secretary and Treasurer, T. Topham, Wharfinger, were re-elected. G. Bowen and S. Barker, Auditors, re-elected. Treasurer directed to deposit in Savings Bank the balance not needed for repairs.

1842. *April* 11. — Annual meeting. The Secretary and Treasurer, Wharfinger and Auditing Committee re-elected. Samuel Engs was elected a Trustee in place of Robert Stevens, resigned. A committee of three was appointed to make repairs, not to exceed $1,000.

*October* 14. — The committee appointed in April last, on repairs, reported, and said report being read, it was voted that the same be accepted, and the committee directed to complete the repairs.

1843. *April* 11. — Annual meeting. The Secretary and Treasurer, Wharfinger and Auditors were re-elected. The committee to repair the wharf directed to receive from Mr. Covill a release of his part of the wharf opposite his shop.

1844. *April* 15. — Annual meeting. David M. Coggeshall was elected Secretary and Treasurer; T. Topham, Wharfinger; S. Barker and G. Bowen, Auditors. Peleg Clarke was elected a Trustee in place of Audley Clarke, deceased. Benjamin A. Mason was elected a Trustee in place of George C. Mason, deceased. The committee reported that a deed from Mr. Covill had been received and left with the Town Clerk to be recorded.

The executor of Henry Bull, deceased, presented a claim of $50 for plastering roof of store; it was contended that he agreed to attend to the plastering of all the stores and to receive from this Corporation $100 in full of all claims against the Long Wharf. G. Bowen and S. Barker were directed to show Mr. Bull's executor the records as to plastering the stores. R. P. Lee and B. Finch, a committee to examine the account of the Committee on

Repairs, and it was voted, that the latter receive the thanks of this Corporation for the faithful discharge of their duties.

*Voted,* That John Stevens and G. Bowen have authority to repair the highway leading from the market to Covill's shop wherever it may require it.

1845. *April* 21. — Annual meeting. D. M. Coggeshall, Secretary and Treasurer, T. Topham, Wharfinger, G. Bowen and S. Barker, Auditors, were re-elected. George G. King was elected Trustee in place of S. A. Robinson, who never accepted. The balance in the treasury ordered to be deposited in the Savings Bank.

1846. *April* 14. — Annual meeting. No quorum. It was recommended that the Treasurer deposit $500 in Savings Bank.

*July* 14. — D. M. Coggeshall, Secretary and Treasurer, T. Topham, Wharfinger, G. Bowen and S. Barker, Auditors, were re-elected. William C. Cozzens was elected a Trustee in place of S. F. Gardner, deceased.

*Voted,* That the Treasurer deposit $250 in Savings Bank and in future, whenever the sum in the treasury amounts to $100 ; the same to be deposited to the credit of the Trustees. J. Stevens and G. Bowen, a committee to make repairs on the highway to Covill's shop, and about the wharf.

1847. *April* 12.—Annual meeting. S. T. Northam was elected Chairman for the year. David M. Coggeshall, Secretary and Treasurer; T. Topham, Wharfinger ; G. Bowen and S. Baker, Auditors ; John Stevens and G. Bowen, Committee on Repairs, were elected. John D. Northam and David G. Cook were elected Trustees, in place of George Engs and Nathaniel S. Ruggles, deceased ; and Samuel Brown was elected in place of R. K. Randolph, removed from town.

J. D. Northam, D. G. Cook, and S. Brown, were appointed a Committee to confer with the proprietors of the north side of Long Wharf, in regard to building a wall in front of their buildings, provided the Trustees will place a good sidewalk the whole distance, and to obtain quitclaims to any individual rights they claim on the south side, except for landing articles for their own use, in case the Trustees should decide to widen the wharf, from Sherman's Wharf to Gravelly Point, say fifteen or twenty feet, and said Committee to report to the next meeting. J. Stevens and G. Bowen to fill any vacancy in the Committee from the Board of Trustees. The Treasurer directed to deposit in Savings Bank the balance in his hands.

*Voted,* That all steamers coming to, or going from Long Wharf, shall shut their dampers, or so regulate their fires as to prevent the fires from the chimneys from doing damage while the boat is within a cable's length, or 120 fathoms of the wharf.

*April* 28.—A letter received by D. G. Cook from Capt. J. J. Comstock, of steamer Bay State, to the Trustees, was presented, asking for higher fenders to be placed at the corners of the wharf, also two fenders of same height midway of the head of the wharf, all to be twelve feet above a usual high tide, or perhaps fifteen feet above. As it is possible there will be a permanent line daily, it is necessary to have every facility for landing and receiving passengers with safety and dispatch. Also asking permission to erect a dolphin, at their own expense, at the north of the wharf; also if something could be done to preserve order during the landing of passengers, their comfort would be promoted. G. Bowen and J. Stevens were appointed a Committee to carry the foregoing into effect, as far as regards the fenders. D. G. Cook and D. M. Coggeshall were appointed a Committee to apply to the Legislature at their next session, for a grant to erect a dolphin, as requested.

*July* 12.—The Committee on widening the wharf reported favorably to the project, which was accepted, the estimated cost $13.15, which was agreed to be carried into effect, and G. Bowen and J. Stevens, the General Committee on Repairs, were instructed to do it, and also to make repairs in the way of sidewalks, as they may think best, on the north side.

*Voted*, That D. G. Cook be a committee to answer the Captain of the Bay State, in regard to building the dolphin; the same and Mr. Finch are instructed to lay before the Council, the request of Capt. Comstock, in relation to the trouble and confusion of landing on the arrival of the boats, and ask them to take such measures as they may deem expedient, and inform Capt. Comstock.

*Voted*, That the Committee on Repairs be authorized to draw on the Treasury, from time to time, as money may be wanted.

The following document was presented :

The undersigned, proprietors of lots on the north side of Long Wharf, in case the Trustees of the lower part of the wharf should adopt the plan of widening it, by building out on the south side, opposite our lots, as far down as the bridge, hereby agree to relinquish all our right to occupy or use the ground in front of our lots respectively, except that we are still to retain all our rights and privileges to the wharf-front, the same as we now enjoy, to the extent of twelve feet north, from the south edge of the wharf, the remainder of the space to be thereafter entirely free and unobstructed as a highway, for the use of the public, the same as any other street in Newport,

32

it being understood that the proprietors of the lots are to keep up the north wall, or line of their lots, on the street or highway, and in such repair that the Trustees may lay a sidewalk on the north side of such highway, if they should see fit to do so, the Trustees to have the right to land all materials for construction or repairs of the wharf, wherever they may think proper.

E. TREVETT,<br>
CALEB S. KNIGHT,<br>
W. D. SOUTHWICK,<br>
her<br>
PENELOPE ✕ KNIGHT,<br>
mark<br>
BENJAMIN EDDY, <i>Agent for S. Gray.</i>

*October* 10. R. K. Randolph, not intending to resign his Trusteeship, the vote electing Samuel Brown in his place was rescinded, and Samuel Brown is elected in place of David M. Coggeshall, deceased. Robert P. Lee was elected Secretary and Treasurer, for the remainder of the year, in place of D. M. Coggeshall, deceased.

It was *Voted*, That the Committee to repair the wharf, be authorized to build such a shed on the end of the wharf as they may think necessary and proper for the accommodation of the steamboat passengers and freight.

1848. *April* 10. Annual Meeting. Stephen T. Northam, Chairman for the ensuing year; Robert P. Lee, Secretary and Treasurer; Theophilus Topham, Wharfinger; S. Barker and G. Bowen, Auditors; John Stevens and G. Bowen, Committee on Repairs, were severally elected. Christopher G. Perry was elected a Trustee in place of Thomas Bush, deceased.

1848. *May* 15.—Mr. Bowen, from the Committee on Repairs, stated that from the damage done by steamboats, in addition to the ordinary wear and tear, to the head of the wharf it would require considerable expense to put it in such order as the steamboats would require, and that, in the opinion of the Committee, the steamboats do not pay sufficient wharfage to warrant the expense of such repairs. After discussion, it was

*Voted*, That John Stevens and George Bowen, the Committee, be authorized to confer with the owners of the steamboats, and endeavor to agree with them for such additional wharfage for the future as may be proper.

Three proprietors of lots on the north side of Long Wharf, west of the bridge, in order that the improvement already carried into effect as far west as the bridge, shall be continued, in order to form a better thoroughfare for the use of the public, have, for that purpose, agreed to keep the space in front of their lots free, reserving their right to the wharf front, leaving the highway twenty-eight feet wide, the proprietors to keep up the wall on the north side of the street, so that a sidewalk may be laid — the Trustees to straighten the south wall as may be necessary, and place curb-stones and a paved gutter on the north side. Their agreement signed by Proprietors, November 12, 1847.

WILLIAM SOUTHWICK.
STEPHEN SOUTHWICK.
JOSEPH SOUTHWICK.

1849. *April* 18.—Annual Meeting. C. Devens was elected a Trustee in place of B. A. Mason, removed to New York ; Robert Sherman, 2d, was elected a Trustee in place of R. K. Randolph, deceased ; J. D. Northam, Chairman ; R. P. Lee, Secretary and Treasurer ; T. Topham, Wharfinger ; S. Barker and G. Bowen, Auditors ; J. Stevens and G. Bowen, Committee on Repairs, were elected for the ensuing year.

The Committee to agree with steamboat owners, in regard to future regulations, made a verbal report, that they had agreed that the Trustees would put the wharf in complete order, and after that the steamboat owners agree to repair all damages they may cause.

The Committee on Repairs made a written report, which was accepted. J. Stevens and G. Bowen, the Committee, presented their bill for services, $300. The bill was read, and no motion taken on it ; but it was *Voted*, That Mr. Stevens and Mr. Bowen be paid $100 each in full compensation.

*Voted*, That from and after this day, no person on any committee shall receive any compensation for his services, unless specially agreed upon at the time of his appointment.

*Voted*, That the Committee on Repairs be requested to make a full and more detailed report of the repairs done under their direction than in the report read to-day, and report to the next meeting.

1850. *April* 10.—Annual Meeting. The Chairman, Secretary and Treasurer, Wharfinger, Auditors, and Committee on Repairs, were all re-elected for the ensuing year.

The Treasurer was directed to deposit in the Savings Bank any moneys he may have on hand.

1851. *April* 10.— Annual meeting. All the Officers of last year were re-elected for the present year.

*Voted*, That Samuel Brown and Christopher G. Perry be a Committee to inquire into the Original Trust of the Trustees of Long Wharf, and Public

School, and also to inquire into the Trust relating to establishing Free Schools, and report at the next meeting.

1852. *April* 10.—Annual Meeting. All the Officers of the past year were again elected for the year.

*Voted*, That the Committee on Repairs be authorized to lay a sidewalk and build a close board fence on the north side of Long Wharf, between Smith & Covill's boatbuilders' shop and the store belonging to the heirs of the late Henry Bull (formerly S. Martin's store), several small sheds having recently been erected on the south side of Long Wharf, eastward of Gravelly Point, which the Trustees deem to be a trespass, and not allowed according to the charter of the Proprietors. The Secretary of the Trustees is requested to represent the matter to the Treasurer of the town, and if such sheds are placed there without a legal right to do so, to request said Treasurer to have them removed.

*August* 9.—Special Meeting. In consequence of the death of Theophilus Topham, Wharfinger, it was

*Voted*, That John Hull be Wharfinger for the balance of the year.

A committee was appointed to inform Mr. Hull of his election, and to ascertain whether his custom-house duties would interfere with his office of Wharfinger.

1853. *April* 14.—Annual Meeting. S. T. Northam, Chairman ; R. P. Lee, Secretary and Treasurer ; John Hull, Wharfinger ; S. Barker and G. Bowen, Auditors ; W. Sherman, G. Bowen and W. C. Cozzens, Committee on Repairs, were elected for the ensuing year.

The Committee on Repairs were requested to advise with the Wharfinger, in regard to rates to be charged for wharfage, and in such other matters as relates to his duty.

The Committee on Repairs are requested to take into consideration the propriety of widening the head of the wharf, on the north side, and to make an estimate of its cost ; also to procure an Act from the State Legislature for that purpose.

1854. *April* 10.—Annual Meeting. The Chairman, Secretary and Treasurer, Wharfinger, and Committee on Repairs, were re-elected for the ensuing year, and Samuel Barker and Robert Sherman, 2d, Auditors.

*Voted*, That the Treasurer inform the Fall River Steamboat Company that after May 1, 1854, they will be required to pay $1,200 for the same accommodation as the past year.

The Committee on Repairs were directed to extend the sidewalk on the north side of the wharf, to the west end of the lower store, and around the corner to the steamboat office.

The same Committee were directed to contract with the Gas Company, to light the wharf, provided they can make a satisfactory arrangement.

*Voted*, That the Committee be authorized to widen the wharf, on the south side, from the Messer estate westward to meet the southeast corner of the present projection, if they deem it expedient to do so.

1855. *April* 12.—Annual meeting. The Chairman, Secretary and Treasurer, Wharfinger, and Committee on Repairs, were re-elected for this year, and D. G. Cook and R. Sherman 2d, Auditors.

*Voted,* That Robert S. Barker and David J. Gould be Trustees, in place of Samuel Barker and Christopher G. Perry, deceased.

*Voted*, That the Committee on Repairs, be directed to light the Long Wharf from Thames Street, to the west end of the wharf.

*Voted*, That the Committee on Repairs be instructed to extend the sidewalk on the north side of the wharf from Washington Street to meet the walk already laid, and to make a walk in all such other places as may require it, on said north side, between said Washington Street and the estate of Miss Richardson.

*Voted*, That the Committee on Repairs, be directed to confer with the proprietors of the Fall River Steamboat Company, and ascertain what alterations and improvements, if any, they require for the accommodations of their boats and passengers, and if they can make a satisfactory bargain for the use of the additional accommodation, to make such alterations and improvements, in their discretion, and draw on the Treasurer for the cost thereof. Mr. Samuel Allen stated that he resided in Middletown, and therefore wished to resign his place as Trustee. It was voted not to fill the place of Mr. Allen until the next meeting.

1856. *April* 10.—Annual meeting. Charles Devens was chosen Chairman for the year, R. P. Lee, Secretary and Treasurer, John Hull, Wharfinger, D. G. Cook and R. Sherman, Auditors, W. C. Cozzens, William Sherman, and G. Bowen, Committee on Repairs. Whereas the Committee on Repairs have erected a new depot building on the end of the wharf, and have insured $3,400 on the same, in the Providence Mutual Company for seven years from October 4, 1855, it is hereby

*Voted*, That the Trustees sanction said act.

*Voted*, That the renting of the new depot be left entirely to the discretion of the Committee on Repairs.

*June* 5. A special meeting. E. W. Lawton, Chairman, *pro tem.;* C. Devens, the standing Chairman, not present at the commencement of the meeting. The Secretary stated that he had called the meeting by request of the Committee on Lighting the Wharf, for the Trustees to receive a communication from the Gas Company, stating the terms on which the Company would light the Wharf. The communication was read, and the Trustees declined the proposal. It was then

*Voted,* That the Committee on Repairs agree with the Gas Company to light ten posts on the wharf, at a price not exceeding $33 per post, per annum ; the Trustees to furnish the posts and lanterns and to keep them in repair.

The Committee on Repairs are authorized and requested to attend to any business that may come before the State Legislature, in which the Trustees of the Long Wharf are interested, and they are empowered to employ counsel if they deem it necessary.

1857. *April* 10. — Annual meeting. All the officers of the past year were re-elected for the present year.

*July* 31. — A special meeting. The Committee on Repairs were authorized to make any contract with the Bay State Company in regard to commutations of freight landed from said Company's boats which they may deem best for the interest of the Trustees.

The Committee on Repairs made a report, that in consequence of an application from the Bay State Company for a lease of the wharf and depot building, they had contracted with the agent of said Company for the use of the head of Long Wharf, for the use of their boats, and for the occupancy of the depot building, they paying at the rate of $1700 per year for the Wharf and building. The lease to continue from July 1, 1857, to July 1, 1859. It was

*Voted,* That the above report be accepted, and that this Board approve and ratify said contract.

1858. *April* 10. — At the annual meeting, all the officers of the past year were re-elected for this year. Judge William R. Staples, who was employed by the Trustees to examine all the papers, books, and acts of the Trustees, from the commencement in 1795 to 1857, in order to determine the exact situation of the Trustees with the Long Wharf and Public School, made his written report.

It was *Voted,* That the said report be accepted, and that the Secretary record the same in the Book of Records of the Trustees and place the original on file.

It was *Voted*, That Robert P. Lee, Secretary and Treasurer, have for his services fifty dollars per year.

*Voted*, That the Treasurer be authorized to place in the Savings Bank of Newport all the money that he has now on hand, and all that he may receive from time to time which he may deem sufficient to deposit.

The Committee on Repairs are authorized to make good and substantial fences across the gaps or openings between the stores on the wharf, west of Gravelly Point, provided the owners of the stores will agree to have them do so.

1859. *April* 18. — Adjourned annual meeting. The officers of last year were re-elected for this year.

*Voted*, That the Committee on Repairs be authorized to continue the services of Mr. John Hull, Wharfinger, after the 1st of July next, in case they arrange with the Bay State Company for commuting the wharfage, at a salary of $100 per year and 20 per cent on all wharfage from other sources.

*Voted*, That the salary of the Secretary and Treasurer be $75 instead of $50 per year.

The amount of funds in Savings Bank, arising from sales of Potter Estate, so called, up to January 1, 1859, was $1,810.56.

*July* 23. — John Hull, Wharfinger, resigned, and John Stevens was appointed Wharfinger for the remainder of the year. The Committee on Repairs to inform Mr. Stevens of his appointment.

The Trustees are indebted to the Report of Judge W. R. Staples, for the following items of the history of the Long Wharf, he having been applied to for an opinion as to the rights and powers of the Trustees, and of their doings since their appointment, under the Act of the General Assembly of January, 1795:

The town of Newport, before the year 1702, owned a wharf where the Long Wharf now is; probably the space was originally left by the purchasers for a public landing place, and that it passed to the town with other undivided lands, when the purchasers relinquished their title to such undivided lands to the towns. Before 1702 there had been a wharf built at this place, a town wharf, which was probably like the original landing place, open to all, and that it was built and maintained at the public expense.

The Wharf in 1702 had gone much to decay, and at that time there was no likelihood of its being repaired again. The town therefore agreed that "them persons in company (as they were called) that shall repair the Wharf, and keep it in repair, shall have the power to choose a Wharfinger, and take the usual custom of wharfage, both for wood and for other things landed thereon." See vote of the town, April 29, 1702.

The object of this vote was to secure to the inhabitants the advantages of a wharf at that place, and, at the same time, to free the town from the expense of repairing it, that burden being shifted from the town to the persons who used it. It had ceased to be a free wharf. A right to collect wharfage on goods landed on it became vested in "them persons in company," and became theirs so long as they kept it in repair. It does not appear that they forfeited that right. See vote of the town, October 3, 1739.

It is inferred from this vote, that the public required greater wharf accommodations at that place, both in width and length, than the old town wharf afforded, and that " them persons in company " were not able or willing to make the outlay required for that purpose. It appears, however, that there were other individuals more venturesome, or more public spirited, who would, and the town, on their petition, granted to them the old town wharf, the unoccupied lands adjoining north and south on Thames Street, the flats westward to Easton's Point, the right to build the wharf across Easton's Point, the flats west of Easton's Point, 800 feet, and the water-right, 45 feet in width, on each side of the wharf.

The petitioners were to agree with the owners of the town wharf, and with the owners of land at Easton's Point. They were to build a wharf 50 feet in width, the whole length from Thames Street, of the granted premises, leaving a channel-way through it into the Cove, with a draw-bridge, on the south side of the wharf. They were to leave a way open 30 feet in width, for the better landing of wood and merchandise. The effect of this vote was a divesting of the town of all right in the old town wharf, in the unoccupied lands on Thames Street, and in the flats to the westward ; and whatever rights they had became invested in the petitioners, for the purposes of the grant, that is, for the purpose of building and maintaining a wharf thereon, of the dimensions before stated.

The petitioners entered into possession of the granted premises ; and that they agreed with the owners of the town wharf, and lands on Easton's Point, may be inferred from other facts in the history of the wharf. They applied to the General Assembly in 1769 for leave to raise £1,350 by lottery, to enable them to complete their agreement with the town of Newport, by extending the wharf 170 feet further west, and also to pave the east end near Thames Street. The petition was granted, but the petitioners were required first to pave the east end of the wharf, and to extend it westward with the balance of the avails of the lottery. As the paving was not done, it is believed the wharf was not extended. By a map of Newport, engraved in 1777, this wharf appears less than 700 feet in length at that time. It therefore appears the proprietors received nothing from the Lottery Grant; they had, however, built a wharf, which if it did not conform exactly with the one contracted to be built, was accepted and used by the public.

There is no evidence that any complaint was ever made against it, by the town. That the wharf was suffered to decay during the War of the Revolution, that it was not repaired during that contest, and that it was ruthlessly destroyed by the British soldiery for fire-wood, while in possession of Newport, are facts beyond controversy. It is not probable that it received much attention during the disastrous period which followed the Revolutionary War, up to the adoption of the Constitution of the United States by the State. No complaint was made, however, about it, at this or any other time, while in their hands, up to 1795.

## THE ACT OF THE GENERAL ASSEMBLY, JANUARY, 1795.

Without petition or complaint from any one, on motion, the Assembly authorized thirty-six persons, citizens of Newport, who are named in the Act, to set forth a scheme to raise by lottery twenty-five thousand dollars.

They were to appoint Managers of the Lottery, who were to give bonds to the General Treasurer for the faithful performance of their Trust as Managers. The powers conferred on them were very broad. How the wharf should be rebuilt, after a title to it had been procured, what kind of a hotel and where to be located, are left to the discretion of these Trustees, who are to act without bond or oath, in discharge of their part of the Trust.

After the wharf and hotel were completed, the Trustees were to apply the rents and profits arising from them to such a Public School for the children of Newport, and in such way and manner, and under such regulations as the Trustees should impose. And the Trust to last through all time, the right of filling vacancies in the number being specially conferred on the survivors. The Board of Trustees originated with the Assembly; the funds which they were to raise and appropriate, were provided by the Assembly. No person

33

was compelled to contribute toward the fund, and no person was compelled to be benefitted by it.

This Act of the Assembly did not affect the title or ownership of the Long Wharf; it did not pretend to do so, nor did the Trustees created by it so understand it, as at their very first meeting they appointed a committee to ascertain by what means they could obtain the foe of it — they seemed to suppose there would be no difficulty in obtaining it at once. This expectation was probably based on the situation of the wharf at that time, requiring to be rebuilt and yielding no adequate return for the use, to which, as Trustees, after being repaired or rebuilt by the avails of the Lottery, they were to apply the net rents and profits.

Their first meeting was on the 14th February, 1795, the proceedings were as per Book of Records of the Trustees, p. 3.

On the 22d March, 1798, the Trustees resolved that they would put the wharf in repair, as soon as they could get a deed of the same; at the same time they invoked the town to aid them in procuring a title to the wharf. Urged by the Trustees, a Town Meeting was held 29th March, 1798, at which a committee was appointed to inquire into the situation of the wharf, and in relation to the title to it. This committee reported to the Town Meeting in April, but the report is not on file.

The subject came before the Town Meeting in June, 1798, and the Town *Resolved*, That inasmuch as the proprietors of that part of the Long Wharf west of Gravelly Point had for many years neglected to comply with the conditions contained in the original grant, and thereby had forfeited all right to the same, and as the rebuilding of the same would be both ornamental and useful to the town, they *voted*, that all the right of the town in the Long Wharf west of Gravelly Point be transferred to the Trustees of the Long Wharf Hotel and Public School Lottery for the purpose, contemplated in the Act of Incorporporation, "*on condition of their rebuilding the same, and keeping it in repair, agreeably to the original grant to the proprietors of the Long Wharf.*"

Six months were allowed *to the proprietors of the other part of the Long Wharf* to put that in repair. The Town Treasurer was directed to make a deed to the Trustees of that part granted, but no such deed is on record.

But when it is shown that the Trustees entered into the possession of the premises voted to them, and continued in possession from that time to the present without legal objection from the proprietors of the Long Wharf, there is every necessary presumption to support the title of the Trustees; and when it is evident that the Trustees, on taking possession, proceeded immediately, with all speed of their times, to rebuild the wharf, and expend large sums of money on it, within sight and cognizance of the proprietors and the town; that on the 23d February, 1799, they appointed a committee to survey the wharf.

On the 5th April they *voted*, To advertise for proposals to rebuild it.

On the 19th July appointed a committee to rebuild it, and on the 11th May, 1801, had expended all their funds derived from the Lottery Grant, and authorized their Treasurer to borrow $1,800 to complete the work.

Any Court of Equity would mulct the complainant in costs, who should now move it to declare no title in the Trustees. A Court of Law, too, would not hesitate to adjudge the title good, under a plea of possession, accompanied with such circumstances. It is therefore assumed that the Trustees, by virtue of this vote of the Town and their acts and possession, and the silence and acquiescence of the proprietors under it, are the owners of that part of the Long Wharf to the westward of Gravelly Point.

The Trustees appointed by the General Assembly, were a body, by the Act which created them, fully authorized to fill vacancies in their Board, and so perpetuate their existence; they had no need of a Charter of Incorporation. But it was not so with the grantees of the Town in 1739; they retained their individual character. Upon the decease of one of them, his interest passed to his heirs, and hence it was that in 1801, when, on the division of the wharf between them and the Trustees, they had become possessed of a valuable property that they felt the necessity, and applied to the General Assembly, for an Act of Incorporation.

In answer to the question of what were the rights of the Trustees under this vote of the town in 1798, it is to be said that they were to hold the part granted, for the purpose contemplated in the Act of Incorporation, on condition of their rebuilding the same and keeping it in repair, agreeably to the original grant to the proprietors of the Long Wharf. They then had it in trust, with no pecuniary advantage to themselves, except what they might have in common with other inhabitants of Newport, in the use of the wharf on paying wharfage, and the advantage arising from a public school. There is no provision in the Trust Deed, or Act of the Assembly, for any pay for any services as Trustees, and of course they are not entitled to any. " Charges and Repairs " are alone to be deducted from the rents and profits. They were to rebuild and keep in repair that part of Long Wharf agreeably to the original grant. If by original grant reference is had to the town vote of 1702, the conditions are very loose; no length or breadth of the wharf is required; simply to repair the old town wharf; and for this they were to receive wharfage for wood and any other thing landed thereon. If reference is meant to the grant of 1739, there is more exactness and certainty in the terms imposed on the grantees. They were to build a wharf 50 feet wide, extending 800 feet west of Gravelly Point from low water mark, a good and substantial wharf, and always leaving 30 feet in width of the said wharf on the south side free and clear of buildings and other incumbrances, for the better landing of wood, lumber, &c., for the benefit of the inhabitants, according to the grant in the year 1702. This reference to the Act of 1702 must have been to bring into view the clause of the Act granting wharfage on wood, and other things landed on the wharf; this however was hardly necessary, as the fee of the land, as far as it could be, was transferred to the grantees.

The Trustees did build a wharf of the required length and width, without any unnecessary delay. They kept it in repair, whenever injured by storm or flood, or accident ; it has been repaired and rebuilt. They were to build a hotel also, from the avails of the lottery grant. This they have not done. It seems from the records before referred to, that more than all the avails from that source were used in repairing the wharf. Taking it for granted that this is so, they surely are not in fault in not building the hotel. All the funds put into their hands is this Lottery Grant. It is not declared which shall be built first, the wharf or the hotel, and if the whole amount expected from that source had been realized, both would probably have been completed.

But they did not, and probably could not, raise it all, and they elected as an object of the greatest importance, the rebuilding of the wharf, rather than the erecting of the hotel. The General Assembly saw their course of proceeding ; the town of Newport, the proprietors of the Long Wharf, were all cognizant of it ; and there is no evidence of any fault found with them by any one. The silence ratified the selection of the Trustees, and justified their proceedings in relation to the wharf and hotel.

### THE ACT OF THE GENERAL ASSEMBLY OF MAY, 1829.

This Act, too, was passed at the mere motion of the Legislature. It is not based on any petition of the Trustees or any other person. The General Assembly assumed, by the first section, to appropriate the west end or head of this wharf, to the exclusive use of the steamers plying between this State and New York, and makes it penal for any other vessel to make any use of that part of the wharf, or of any part of the sides so as to interfere with that exclusive use of the head by said steamers. The object of this Act is very apparent ; it was to facilitate steamboat communication between Newport and New York.

The wharf being a public wharf, as before stated, in the sense there intimated, these steam packets had a right in common with all other vessels to stop at it, without an Act of the Legislature ; it might not be in the power of the owners of such a wharf to give a preference in the use of the wharf, to one class of vessels over another. The advantages which would result to the State from such a line of steamboat communication, and the increased safety to passengers on such a route by such legislation, might induce the General Assembly to grant this power to a wharf owner. A similar exclusive use of the ferry wharves in this State is vested in the ferry owners.

The Trustees, by the second section, are empowered to make a contract with the owners or agents of such steamers, for the exclusive use of the head of the wharf ; for it is only when such contract is in force, that it is penal for other vessels to use the head of the wharf. Being so empowered, it would seem necessarily to draw after it the power to make such further limitations to the use of the wharf as a public wharf, as would ensure the successful use of the part exclusively contracted for, and without which this would be imperfect. This would, therefore, authorize the Trustees to shut up the thirty-foot way at the head of the wharf ; the language of the Act is broad enough to embrace it : " The west end of the Long Wharf in Newport, to wit," across the head thereof, is exclusively appropriated to these steamers, " and the power to contract with the agents or owners for the head of the wharf as aforesaid."

The Trustees are the legal owners of the wharf in question, not only having the right as wharf owners, but by the Act of their appointment, it is their duty to collect wharfage on wood and any other goods that are landed on it, whether they belong to the State, to the City, or to individuals. They have the same right over the wharf, and its use within the conditions contained in the Act appointing them, and subsequent Acts of the Legislature, as other wharf owners have over their wharves.

Between February, 1803, and February, 1805, deeds were made by the Treasurer of the Trustees, of lots on the north side of the wharf west of Gravelly Point, by virtue of a Resolution of the Assembly, February, 1803. The resolution is in the handwriting of John L. Boss, Jr., Clerk of the House, but there is no petition on file, nor is it referred to.

We now continue the report from the Record.

1860. *April* 10. — At the annual meeting the officers of the last year were all re-elected.

1861. *April* 11. — At the annual meeting the officers of the past year were all re-elected.

*Voted*, To remit the wharfage bill against ship Mechanic, in consequence of injury sustained by that vessel while laying at the wharf.

*May* 23. — At a special meeting, C. Devens, chairman,

It was *Voted*, That a petition be presented to the General Assembly at the May session, asking for power to lease the Long Wharf, and dock adjoining, to any railroad company which may build a railroad from Fall River to Newport. W. C. Cozzens and D. G. Cook were appointed a committee to make such alterations as may be desirable to the petition read before the meeting and to present the same to the General Assembly.

1862. *January* 18. — At a meeting, William C. Cozzens, Chairman, Benjamin Finch, as President of the Newport & Fall River Railroad Company, presented a communication asking the terms for a long lease of the wharf to the Railroad Company; whereupon it was

*Voted*, That the wharf be leased at $1400 per annum on a long lease, the Railroad Company to keep it in repair and pay all expenses, with leave to enlarge the wharf as they may think proper.

R. Sherman, S. Engs and S. Brown were appointed the committee. John Stevens was elected Secretary and Treasurer for the remainder of the year in place of Robert P. Lee, deceased, at the salary of the former Secretary and Treasurer, *pro rata*. The Treasurer is directed to deposit the funds, now on hand, in the Savings Bank, if interest will be allowed from to-day. $50 to be allowed the heirs of R. P. Lee, as his portion of the salary for the year. Capt. Charles E. Hammett was elected a Trustee in the place of R. P. Lee, deceased.

*April* 14. — At the annual meeting, B. Finch, Chairman, and J. Stevens, Secretary. D. G. Cook was elected Chairman and J. Stevens, Secretary and Treasurer. . The Committee on Repairs of last year and the Auditors were re-elected. The Treasurer presented his account, in which he credits $1210.-89 as the balance received from the administrator of R. P. Lee, deceased, late Treasurer, and continues the account to this date, showing a balance in his hands of $108.69 now in the hands of Mr. Stevens, due the Trust.

A verbal report was made by the Committee to lease the Long Wharf, that the lease had been drawn but not yet executed, being left in the hands of the Railroad Company for consideration; subsequently the lease being duly executed, a copy of it is herewith presented, as follows:

## COPY OF LEASE OF LONG WHARF, NEWPORT,

TO

## NEWPORT & FALL RIVER RAILROAD COMPANY.

JUNE 5, 1862.

*Whereas*, The General Assembly of the State of Rhode Island and Providence Plantations, at their May Session, A. D. eighteen hundred and sixty-one, passed a certain act, a portion whereof is in the words and figures following, namely, " It is enacted by the General Assembly, as follows:

" SECTION 1st. The Trustees of the Long Wharf in Newport are hereby authorized to make and execute a lease of the exclusive use of their Wharf and Docks in Newport for such time, and upon such terms and conditions as they may think proper, to any Railroad Corporation which may construct a Railroad from Newport to Fall River."

" *And Whereas*, At a meeting of said Trustees of Long Wharf and Free School, held at Newport, in the State aforesaid, on Saturday, January the eighteenth, A. D. eighteen hundred and sixty-two, it was voted as follows:

" That the Wharf be leased at *fourteen hundred dollars* per annum, on a long lease, and that a committee of three be appointed to make a contract for a long lease to the Newport and Fall River Railroad Company ; the Railroad to keep it in repair and pay all expenses, with leave to enlarge the Wharf as they may think proper. Robert Sherman, Samuel Engs, and Samuel Brown, to be the Committee."

*Now, therefore*, this Indenture, made at Newport, in the County of Newport and State of Rhode Island, aforesaid, on the fifth day of June, A. D. eighteen hundred and sixty-two, by and between the Trustees of the Long Wharf and Free School aforesaid, by Robert Sherman, Samuel Engs, and Samuel Brown, a committee duly authorized and appointed for this purpose, as aforesaid, of the first part, and the Newport and Fall River Railroad Company, a Corporation legally created by act of the General Assembly of our said State of Rhode Island, of the second part, *Witnesseth*, That said parties of the first part, for and in consideration of the rents and covenants herein reserved and contained, on the part of said parties of the second part, to be paid and performed, do hereby demise, lease, and to farm let, unto said parties of the second part, the exclusive use of said Long Wharf and the Docks thereof, and all the right, title, and interest of said parties of the first part in and to the same premises, with full leave, liberty, and privilege to enlarge said Wharf, at the cost of said parties of the second part, in any manner and to any extent in or to which it would be lawful for said parties of the first part, at any time hereafter, if this lease had not been made, to enlarge the same.

*To have and to hold* said premises, with the appurtenances thereof, unto said parties of the second part, their successors and assigns, for and during the term of *one hundred years* from the first day of July, A. D. eighteen hundred and sixty-two, with the privilege and right, to said parties of the second part, their successors and assigns, at their own option to renew said lease, at the expiration of the term aforesaid, for the further term of *one hundred years*, at the same rent and upon the same conditions herein reserved and contained ; yielding and paying therefor, during said term, the annual rent of *one thousand and four hundred dollars*, in equal quarterly payments in each and every year of said term, the first of which payments is to be made on the first day of October, A. D. eighteen hundred and sixty-two.

*Provided,* That if said rent, or any part thereof, shall be behind and unpaid on any day of payment, as hereinbefore specified, and shall remain unpaid for the space of six calendar months thereafter ; or if default shall be made in any of the covenants, on the part of said parties of the second part herein contained, and such default shall continue for the space of six calendar months, then said parties of the first part, or their successors, may, at their option, and without previous notice, or demand, determine this lease, and re-enter upon said demised premises, and the same repossess as of their former estate.

*And said parties of the second part*, for themselves, their successors, and assigns, do covenant with said parties of the first part, and their successors, in manner following, namely :

*That they*, said parties of the second part, their successors and assigns, shall and will pay the rent aforesaid, in manner aforesaid ; *And will*, at their own cost, at all times during the continuance of this lease, keep said demised premises, and all enlargements and additions thereto, which may be hereafter made, in good, sound, and serviceable repair. *And will*, yearly, and every year during the continuance of this lease, pay and discharge all taxes, assessments, and levies, which, at any time during said period, shall be lawfully taxed, assessed, or imposed on said premises, or on any part thereof, or on said parties of the first part, or their successors, on account of the same. *And will* pay all expenses, costs, and charges, of every kind whatsoever, incident to the ownership of said premises, or which said parties of the first part would themselves otherwise be bound and liable to pay. *And will* always, during said term, light said wharf, in the night time, with gas lights (or with such other lighting apparatus and material as for the time being may from time to time be found most proper and advantageous) from Thames Street down to the west end of said Wharf, to an equal degree and to the same extent, in all respects, as said wharf has heretofore been lighted by said parties of the first part, or by their tenants.

*Provided,* That whenever, hereafter, some other convenient and commodious street or way shall be provided and established for public travel to and from the premises hereby demised, then such street or way shall be lighted by said parties of the second part, their successors and assigns, in manner as aforesaid, and the obligation to light said wharf, as above said, shall cease and determine.

*And will,* at the end of said term or of the renewal thereof, or other sooner termination of this lease, peaceably surrender said demised premises to said parties of the first part, or their successors, in good order and repair.

*And said parties of the first part,* for themselves and their successors, do hereby covenant and agree to and with said parties of the second part, their successors and assigns, as follows:

*That they,* said parties of the second part, may, at any time during the continuance of this lease, enlarge said wharf hereby demised, at the cost of them, said parties of the second part, in any manner and to any extent, in or to which said parties of the first part, as the owners and occupiers of said premises, might lawfully enlarge the same.

*That they,* said parties of the second part, their successors or assigns, shall, if they so devise, renew this lease for a second term of *one hundred years,* as hereinbefore provided and set forth.

*And that they,* said parties of the second part, performing their covenants herein contained, and paying the rent as aforesaid, shall and may lawfully, quietly, and peaceably hold and occupy said afore demised premises for and during said term of *one hundred years,* and for and during the renewal hereof, herein provided, without lawful let or hindrance of any person whatever.

*In witness whereof,* said parties of the first part have caused these presents

34

to be executed by their Committee aforesaid; and said parties of the second part have caused their President, Benjamin Finch, to affix their corporate seal hereunto and to subscribe his name hereunto for the perfect execution hereof, on this fifth day of June, A. D. eighteen hundred sixty-two.

ROB'T SHERMAN, ⎫  [L. S.]
SAMUEL ENGS, ⎬ *Committee.* [L. S.]
SAM. BROWN, ⎭  [L. S.]

Executed and delivered in }
presence of

FRANCIS B. PECKHAM, Jr.

NEWPORT & FALL RIVER RAILROAD Co.

By BENJ. FINCH, *President.*

STATE OF RHODE ISLAND, &c. }
Newport, ss.

NEWPORT, June 5th, 1862.

Personally appeared the aforenamed Robert Sherman, Samuel Engs, and Samuel Brown, and acknowledged the foregoing instrument to be the free act and deed of themselves, and of the Trustees of the Long Wharf and Free School in Newport.

Also personally appeared the aforenamed Benjamin Finch, President of the Newport and Fall River Railroad Company, and acknowledged said instrument to be the free act and deed of said Railroad Company.

Before me,

FRANCIS B. PECKHAM, JR.,
*Justice of Peace.*

*April* 14. — Seth W. Macy was elected a Trustee in place of Peleg Clarke, deceased.

*Voted,* That a committee be appointed to purchase a suitable lot for a new school house, to be erected in the First Ward by the Long Wharf Trustees; that said Committee confer with the Joint Committee of the City and School Committee as to the location of said lot, and invite them to furnish plans of a school house such as they would approve.

Samuel Engs, Robert Sherman and David J. Gould were appointed the committee and authorized to draw on the Treasurer for the amount required to pay for the lot, and when purchased they are requested to report to the Trustees with such plans for the proposed building as they may obtain from the Joint Committee before mentioned.

*May* 20. — At a special meeting of the Trustees, the Commiteee appointed in relation to the proposed new school house, to be erected in the First Ward, made a report, stating that they had purchased a lot 100 feet square, on the corner of Third and Willow Street for $850, and had paid for the same ; they also presented plans and drawings of a school house, together with a letter from George C. Mason, in which he estimates the cost of such a building at $9,000. Mr. Finch offered the following resolution, which was passed.

*Voted*, That the plans for a school house, drawn by George C. Mason and approved by the Committee, be adopted, and that the same Committee be continued in power, and they are requested to have specifications drawn in accordance therewith, and that they advertise in the newspapers, inviting sealed proposals for building said school house, and when such proposals are received they are to be opened and read only in the presence of the Trustees, at a meeting to be called by the Committee for that purpose.

John Stevens was re-appointed Wharfinger until the lease of the Long Wharf to the Railroad Company goes into effect.

*June* 26. — At a special meeting, the committee appointed in relation to the proposed new school house in the First Ward, presented the proposals which had been received, and were opened in the presence of the Trustees. After debate it was

*Voted*, That the proposals be returned to the Committee as being entirely above our means, and that they be required to ascertain from the architect in what manner the cost of the building can be reduced to a sum not exceeding $11,000, to include heating apparatus for the house, desks, desk-seats, grading and fencing the ground, and everything complete for the reception of the scholars, also to include lightning rods.

1862. *July* 3. — At a Special Meeting, D. G. Cook, Chairman, a Report was made from the Committee in relation to the proposed new School House, with reduced estimates, but still showing that the house could not be built upon anything near the original plan, even with the reduction proposed, for much, if anything, less than $13,000, to cover every expense. Mr. G. C. Mason being present, explained what the proposed reductions would do towards lessening the cost, and stated that he expected some further proposals from New York ; and it was stated by the Committee that another proposal, for the whole building complete, might be expected to be made, in addition to the proposals already received, and which have been to-day laid before the meeting. On motion of Robert Sherman, it was

*Voted*, That the School House shall be built in accordance with the reduced plan presented, provided the whole expense does not exceed $13,000, to include everything required to make it complete in all respects.

That this meeting will adjourn to meet again on Wednesday next, July 9, at 3 P. M., to hear the Report of the Committee, as to any additional proposals to build the School House, and also as to whether a loan from any bank in this city can be obtained, of the amount required to complete the building, upon a pledge of the property, together with the rent arising from the lease of the Long Wharf to the Newport and Fall River Railroad Co.

*July* 9. — At a Special Meeting of the Trustees, a written report was made by the Building Committee, showing the various proposals which had been made under the reduced estimates, whereupon it was

*Resolved*, That the Building Committee be, and they are hereby, authorized to contract with Philip Simmons to build the proposed School House, in accordance with the plans and specifications adopted by the Trustees, for a sum not exceeding $11,900 ; and to contract for the heating and providing desks and seats for said School House, on the most favorable terms.

*Voted*, That Samuel Engs, David J. Gould, and Robert Sherman, be the Building Committee, and they are hereby authorized to make all contracts and terms of payment, and to draw on the Treasurer, from time to time, for such sums of money as may be necessary to fulfil the contracts, and for other purposes connected therewith.

*Voted*, That the Treasurer be hereby authorized to withdraw from the Savings Bank the amount realized from the sale of the old Long Wharf Free School House, and its accumulations, which are now on special deposit in the Savings Bank, and to apply the same, and other funds in said Savings Bank, towards the building of the new School House.

*Voted*, That the Treasurer be, and he is hereby, empowered and authorized to hire, on account of the Trustees, such sum or sums of money as may be necessary, after using the funds now on hand, or belonging to the Trustees, to pay the orders of the Building Committee, and to give his note or notes therefor.

*Voted*, That the Chairman and William C. Cozzens be a Committee to arrange for an address, containing an historical account of the Long Wharf and its Free School, to be delivered at the dedication of the new School House.

The Chairman reported that he had prevailed upon Governor Wm. C. Cozzens, to deliver an address on the occasion of the dedication of the new School House, and that he had prepared an abstract from the records, to be printed with the address as an appendix.

1863. *April* 13. — At the Annual Meeting, David G. Cook was elected Chairman for the ensuing year ; John Stevens, Secretary and Treasurer ; D. G. Cook and Robert Sherman, Auditors. Charles E. Hammett, Jr., was elected a Trustee, in place of Joseph Paddock, deceased.

The Building Committee made a verbal report, that the School House was nearly completed, with the exception of the desks and seats, and they were authorized and requested, in concert with the Committee appointed July 9, 1862, to arrange for an address to be delivered on the occasion of the dedication, and to make all necessary arrangements for the dedication, to take place about the 20th of May. The said Committee to cause five hundred copies of the proceedings at the dedication, together with an abstract from the records, to be published. Charles E. Hammett, Jr., was added to this Committee.

The Treasurer's account for the year was presented, received, and accepted, showing a balance of forty cents in his hands, and an overdraft on the R. I. Union Bank of $1,211.82.

Adjourned.

At a Special Meeting of the Trustees, on Wednesday, May 20, 1863, at 2.30 o'clock P. M., at the New School House, previous to the dedication services, it was—

*Voted and resolved,* That Governor William C. Cozzens be and he is hereby authorized and requested, in his address, to make a formal presentation to the Mayor and City Council, of the possession, use, and occupancy of the New School House recently erected on Third and Willow Street for a Public School of the City of Newport; the said building to continue under their entire control so long as the said city authorities shall maintain a Public School therein.

*Voted and resolved,* That David G. Cook, Chairman of the Board of Trustees, is hereby authorized and requested to present to the Mayor of the City of Newport the keys of the said School House.

*Voted,* That a marble tablet, containing the names of the present Trustees, be placed on the wall of the New School House, together with the names of the Committee, the Architect, and Builders, with date of its erection ; and that Benjamin Finch and William C. Cozzens be a Committee to attend to it.

*Voted,* That this Board now adjourn to attend the dedication services.

## NAMES OF TRUSTEES OF THE LONG WHARF FROM 1795 TO 1862.

*The first ninety-six were appointed by the General Assembly of Rhode Island. All others were appointed by the Board at their Annual or Special Meetings.*

| Appointed. | Names. | Died, resigned, or removed. |
|---|---|---|
| January, 1795. | Henry Marchant, | died, August 30, 1796. |
| " | George Gibbs, | removed July,.1811, f'm t'n. |
| " | George Champlin, | died July 8, 1811. |
| " | Christopher Champlin, | died April 25, 1805. |
| " | James Robinson, | resigned August 14, 1814. |
| " | Peleg Clarke, | died December 3, 1803. |
| " | Henry Sherburne, | resigned July 8, 1807. |
| " | John Bours, | resigned July 8, 1807. |
| " | Oliver Warner, | died November, 1799. |
| " | John Handy, | resigned July 8, 1807. |
| " | Francis Malbone, | died July 8, 1811. |
| " | Daniel Mason, | died September 24, 1797. |
| " | Ethan Clarke, | died September 30, 1833. |
| " | Christopher Fowler, | died April 12, 1830. |
| " | Simeon Martin, | resigned October 11, 1819. |
| " | Thomas Dennis, | resigned April 10, 1813. |
| " | John L. Boss, | died October 11, 1824. |
| " | Samuel Vernon, Jr. | died April 13, 1835. |
| " | Christopher Ellery, | died December 2, 1840. |
| " | Christopher G. Champlin, | resigned July 8, 1811. |
| " | William Ellery, Jr. | resigned April 10, 1811. |
| " | Daniel Lyman, | rem'd f'm town July 8,1811. |
| " | Isaac Senter, | died Dec. 20, 1799. |
| " | Benjamin Mason, | died. |
| " | Aaron Sheffield, | died Octocer.4, 1796, |
| " | William Littlefield, | died November 21, 1822. |
| " | Silas Dean, | died October 11, 1819. |
| " | Audley Clarke, | died April 15, 1844. |
| " | Constant Taber, | died February 15, 1827. |
| " | Caleb Gardner, | died October 26, 1806. |
| " | Nathan Bebec, | died in Nantucket. |
| " | Moses Seixas, | died July 8, 1811. |

| Appointed. | Names, | Died, resigned, or removed. |
| --- | --- | --- |
| January, 1795. | Nicholas Taylor, | died April 13, 1829. |
| " | Walter Channing, | rem'd f'm town July, 1815. |
| " | Archibald Crary, | died in New York. |
| " | Robert Rogers, | died September 14, 1835. |
| July 8, 1811. | Christopher Rhodes, | resigned April 10, 1815. |
| " | William Engs, | resigned April 10, 1815. |
| " | William Marchant, | resigned August 19, 1814. |
| " | Stephen T. Northam, | died April 10, 1856. |
| " | Jonathan Bowen, | rem'd f'm t'n Apr. 13, 1829. |
| July 11, 1811. | Robert Robinson, | died April 13, 1829. |
| " | Edward Martin, | resigned January 7, 1822. |
| August 19, 1814. | Gilbert Chace, | died January 10, 1820. |
| " | John G. Whitehorne, | resigned April 10, 1826. |
| April 10, 1815. | William Ennis, | died April 9, 1832. |
| " | Benjamin Hadwen, | died January 10, 1837. |
| " | John R. Sherman, | resigned January 8, 1821. |
| " | William C. Gardner, | resigned January 7, 1822. |
| July 10, 1815. | William Hunter, | rem'd f'm t'n Apr. 10, 1826. |
| October 11, 1816. | Lewis Rousmaniere, | died July 10, 1820. |
| October 11, 1819. | George Engs, | died April 12, 1847. |
| " | S. Fowler Gardner, | died August 2, 1845. |
| January 10, 1820. | Stephen Gould, | rem'd f'm t'n Apr. 13, 1829. |
| January 8, 1821. | Benjamin Pierce, | died July 14, 1823. |
| " | James Stevens, | rem'd f'm t'n Apr. 14, 1828. |
| January 7, 1822. | Nathaniel S. Ruggles, | died April 12, 1847. |
| " | Edward W. Lawton, | |
| July 14, 1823. | Robert Stevens, Jr. | resigned April 11, 1842. |
| October 11, 1824. | David King, | died January 10, 1837. |
| April 10, 1826. | Nicholas G. Boss, | died January 10, 1837. |
| April 9, 1827. | Richard K. Randolph, | removed from town. |
| April 12, 1827. | David M. Coggeshall, | died October 10, 1847. |
| April 14, 1828. | James B. Phillips, | died April 8, 1833. |
| April 13, 1829 | Henry Bull, | resigned April, 1831. |
| " | Stephen Bowen, | died July 13, 1829. |
| " | Thomas Bush, | died April 10, 1848. |
| " | John Stevens, | |
| July 13, 1829. | George Bowen, | |
| April 12, 1830. | Samuel Allen, | resigned April 12, 1855. |
| April 11, 1831. | Richard K. Randolph, | died April 18, 1849. |
| " | Isaiah Crooker, | |

| Appointed. | Names. | Died, resigned, or removed. |
| --- | --- | --- |
| April 9, 1832. | George C. Mason, | died Dec. 23, 1843. |
| April 8, 1833. | John V. Hammett, | |
| September 14, 1835. | Robert. Lee, | died June, 1861. |
| January 10, 1837. | Benjamin Finch, | |
| " | Samuel Barker, | died April 12, 1855. |
| " | William Sherman, | |
| April 11, 1842. | Samuel Ings, | |
| April 15, 1844. | Peleg Clarke, | died March, 1862. |
| " | Benjamin A. Mason, | removed from town. |
| April 21, 1845. | George T. King, | |
| July, 14, 1846. | William C. Cozzens, | |
| April 12, 1847. | John H. Northam, | |
| " | David G. Cook, | |
| October 10, 1847. | Samuel Brown, | |
| April 10, 1848. | Christopher G. Perry, | died April 12, 1855. |
| April 18, 1849. | Charles Devens, | died April, 1863. |
| " | Robert·Sherman, 2d, | |
| April 12, 1855. | Robert S. Barker, | |
| " | David J. Gould, | |
| April 10, 1856. | Samuel Allen, Jr. | |
| " | Joseph Paddock, Jr. | died March, 1863. |
| January 18, 1862. | Charles E. Hammett, | |
| April 14, 1862. | Seth W. Macy, | |
| April 13, 1863, | Charles E. Hammett, Jr. | |